2.50

P9-ASC-547

A CRITERION BOOK
FOR YOUNG PEOPLE

miriam

miriam

by AIMÉE SOMMERFELT

translated by Mrs. Pat Shaw Iversen

CRITERION BOOKS · NEW YORK

First American edition, 1963
Copyright © 1963 by Criterion Books
Library of Congress Catalog Card Number: 63-10425
This book was originally published in 1960
by Glydendal Norak Forlag, Oslo, Norway.
Manufactured in the United States of America

CONTENTS

41723

NAZARETH LIBRARY
NAZARETH. KENTUCKY

miriam

1 *MIRIAM*

When Hanne came to Oslo she did not meet Miriam right
away even though she seemed to run into her everywhere
in that big, old house. The name *Miriam* had been carved
over one of the hooks in the front hall as if to make clear
to everybody that here her coat had hung, and here it would
hang again one day. In the pretty room up in the attic, which
was Hanne's now, Miriam was present like a shadow one
could never lay hands on, even though it could not have
been many days since she had been sitting in the armchair
by the bed, and had walked on the pale, thick rug which

11

covered the floor. But who she was and what she looked like, Hanne did not know, and there was no one who could tell her.

When Hanne thought of her own narrow room in Trondheim, and compared it with Miriam's luxuriously big one where she could walk about, not just sleep and sit, she felt a pang of conscience, as though she had driven someone out who, by rights, belonged there. And, all the while, as she helped her father, Hanne had the most untimely desire to escape from all the bustle of moving in. She wanted to go up to Miriam's room and sit quietly. Instead she had to gaze at the disorder around her. There was so much to do. She could not leave the work and daydream in the attic.

Shoving aside an empty packing case so she could see her father's face, she asked, "Papa, how old is she, this Miriam?"

"About as old as you are, I think," said her father absent-mindedly, while he climbed up a stepladder.

The room was overflowing with furniture and packing cases. Those who had lived here before had left all their furniture behind, and now the tables and chairs of two families stood jumbled together looking as though they could never be united.

Hanne went from room to room, studying them, trying to imagine what these people had been like who, until so recently, had lived in this funny old house. It seemed to her that she came across them in every corner, that their habits had left marks on the worn floors. But if she asked her parents about them, they turned away and started talking about something else. There are so many other things to talk about when one is moving into a strange house.

The brass nameplate on the front door had been screwed off, and an unpainted square marked the spot where it had stood. It lay on the windowsill. Hanne had seen it herself: *Engineer S. Frænkel* it said. Beside it lay their own nameplate which was to go up: *Foreman Hj. Hoygard.* Her father had not gotten around to screwing it on yet, there was more of a hurry to get rid of the old one.

"Must we really keep *all* their furniture?" asked Mrs. Hoygard. "Why, those big chairs alone devour all the space . . ."

"You know we have to," replied Mr. Hoygard, a little impatiently.

Hanne's blue eyes roamed from the huge space-filling chairs to her father at the top of the stepladder.

"Why can't we put them up in the attic, Papa? Some of them at any rate."

Mr. Hoygard tried in vain to find a space for one of his own pictures in the midst of all the strange ones crowded together.

"Because they are to look as if they are ours," he said. "Remember that, if anyone asks. They are ours!"

"What's the name of this house?" Hanne tried to approach the question from another angle.

"At the factory I hear they call it 'The Old Court.' "

"But surely it can't have been called that all the time. When it was new and everything, I mean. What was this house called when it was new?"

There was often a logic to Hanne's questions that was exasperating.

"Oh, then it probably had the same name as the factory. It's the first and oldest of the houses down here."

That she could see. The rooms were large and deep, with broad, worn thresholds, and tall, narrow windows, as there often are in old houses. In those days, people believed that light could only come in if the windows were slanted. The curtains were so long that they trailed on the floor like bridal veils.

"Papa, why have the Frænkels left?"

"Left? . . . left? Dreadful the way you are poking and prying. Hold this hammer for me instead." Hanne took the hammer.

"How many children do they have?"

"Hanne, you are very curious."

"Is there anything wrong with that?"

"In times like these, yes. The less one knows these days, the better!"

Of course! It was the war. She ought to have known.

War had come to Hanne as a rush of unceasing, confusing talk right over her head. She had seen it all begin in her parents' changed, bewildered faces. Parents' faces are not usually bewildered, she knew that, but this sudden, brutal war, sweeping a country that had been at peace for more than a hundred years, took them by surprise. They couldn't always hide their disgust and shock and fright, even in front of Hanne who turned to them for comfort.

For two tense months the campaign had lasted, Norwegian soldiers retreating slowly through burning valleys. Two months full of atrocities, of bombed towns and homeless people. Until surrender came. Then, one day, the streets were swarming with green-clad soldiers who ordered the Norwegians about. The campaign was over. Norway was occupied.

The war. How she hated that cruel, stinging word. Hated, hated, hated.

Of course, it was the war, turning everything and everybody upside down. The less one knew these days, the better. Everybody said so.

Apparently her father decided to answer her question after all.

"How many children the Frænkels have? Three, I believe. A girl your age, a grown daughter and a boy of eleven."

"A girl my age? Turned sixteen? Then that must be Miriam!"

"Exactly."

Mrs. Hoygard came in from the kitchen.

"Must it take two of you to hang those pictures? Can't one of you help me by carrying in the boxes of kitchen utensils from the porch? But don't leave the door open. Brrr! I think it's colder here in Oslo than up north in Trondheim!" Mrs. Hoygard's homely voice seemed to sweep the war out of the room.

Hanne started carrying in the boxes. At one end of the deep parlor a long console mirror hung out from the wall at an angle, reflecting everyone who came by from top to toe. Hanne, who was accustomed to seeing herself in a small,

41723

NAZARETH LIBRARY
NAZARETH, KENTUCKY

square mirror, so that she had to piece the squares together in her mind if she wanted to find out about her whole self, couldn't resist twirling around each time she carried a load out into the kitchen. It was fun to watch herself walking by, even though boxes were almost all she could see. She didn't know whether the slanting mirror made her taller or whether she really had grown lately. Carefully she put the boxes down in a large, heavy chair, closed the door against the cold Oslo air, and studied herself in the mirror. When she wasn't being curious, she was wrapped up in herself.

Miriam has also stood here and looked at herself, she thought.

Hanne's blonde hair seemed to glow in the half-dark parlor. Short, thick and glossy, it clung softly to her head— "like feathers on a bird's breast," her father used to say. "The *only* orderly thing about Hanne," her mother would add. Anyway, my hair's pretty, Hanne thought, no matter what.

Funny the way one changed so from birthday to birthday. Her figure went in-and-out in the right places, wasn't so stupid and childishly flat any longer. She put her hands on her hips and twirled around.

"Why Hanne! Why are you here, looking at yourself in the mirror when we have so much to do?"

"My skirt is too short, Mother. See how much I've grown."

"It's only the mirror that makes you look so tall."

Mrs. Hoygard lined up beside her daughter and Hanne saw how her mother's round figure stretched and became slim in the glass.

"Oh." Hanne's voice echoed her disappointment. "And I thought I'd grown." She threw a wet dustcloth at the mirror.

"Hanne, shame. That is not our mirror. You must be careful."

"Mother, what *is* all the secrecy about these Frænkels?"

"If you, for example, would work a little more and fuss a little less. . . ."

As far back as Hanne could remember she had heard: "Don't fuss, don't ask questions, sit still, be calm." She had heard these admonitions so often that she scarcely heard them any more. Heard them from tired voices, from vexed voices, from impatient voices, depending on the mood of her parents.

But today she felt that the rebuke was more unjust than usual. She *had* been working hard ever since she came home from school, and besides she didn't fuss any more. She was too old for such childishness. She *walked* up stairs one step at a time, she *sat* in chairs, didn't ride them. She didn't pry and fuss any more, except when there was as much to ask about as there was here. She *was* calm. It was just that the family hadn't yet discovered that she had grown up.

Besides, they could show a *little* confidence in her, even if there was a war on. Why must they hide everything about the Frænkels from her?

Her mother carried the tea things into the parlor, and cleared a space on one of the tables. They sat in the big chairs, which felt queer and strange, and ate their supper. There were empty boxes and wrapping paper on all sides.

A thousand questions were on the tip of Hanne's tongue, but she knew she shouldn't ask them in times like these, and she was also struggling to hang on to her sense of injury, which, she knew from the past, would disappear as soon as she had eaten.

The picture her father had wrestled with was hanging in place, looking squeezed-in and strange, as the crowded furniture did.

"Everyone that comes here will be able to tell that this is the furniture of two families," said Hanne after a long silence. "You'll have to make a sofa corner in the big dining room if it's not to show."

"That's a bright idea," said her father, and Hanne's annoyance evaporated like dew before the sun. She loved praise. Soon afterwards she sat on her father's lap, kissing him goodnight. He had sawdust in his hair, and his unshaven cheeks scratched her skin.

"Tell me about the girl who lived in my room, Papa! As much as you can."

"But I don't know anything about her, my child. Now off to bed and sleep well. If you should be afraid of the dark up there, just knock on the floor for me. I'll be right up."

"I won't be afraid, Papa." She had chosen the attic room herself because it was so unlike her own in Trondheim. "I've looked forward to going to bed all day. Goodnight you two!"

She ran up the steep attic stairs, where the steps were so shallow that she stubbed her toes. Once inside the room, she stood with her back to the door and looked around her.

The bed stood in a niche, and beside it was a little armchair, and a rug that was thick and soft to bare toes. The lamps had a special charm so that one wanted to see them lit. Desk, bookcase, heater—the only room in the house without too much furniture. Here it was cozy, homelike, lived in, as if Miriam, who was no longer here, had just gotten up from the chair and walked out of the door.

Hanne went over to the window. It was a cold spring and the sky looked icy. On all sides the cement buildings of the factory pressed in on the old house, squeezing the garden into a tiny square of flower beds, with enough room for a few apple trees which were full of buds. Straight ahead, the view opened over Bentse Bridge and the Aker River. The city seemed large and distant in the evening mist. In Trondheim the houses were low and the streets wide; there the starry skies dominated the scene.

Hanne thought how another girl had stood gazing out over the housetops from this attic room, and how one day she had pinned up a picture of Cary Grant, which still hung on the curtain. And she never dreamed that soon a completely strange girl would stand in her place, and move Cary a little so she could admire him better.

Then maybe she had gone over and sat down at the desk.

Of all the furnishings in this wonderful room, Hanne admired the desk most. Small, graceful, it was the sort of desk that appears to stand on tiptoe, not sharp-edged as most writing tables are. It had no corners, everything on it was rounded, even the legs.

Hanne lowered the blackout curtain, sat down at the

desk, and lit the lamp. Her school books lay in a pile on the light gray desk top and they looked spotted and impudent, like self-invited guests in a strange parlor. On a shelf to the right stood a number of old school books that were also full of spots, but even so, the books belonged. They were not intruders.

Refsdal's *Atlas*. Brekke's *English Reader*. Exactly the same books that she herself had used last year. She began to examine the books. Their jackets had been removed and inside there was no name to identify the owner but there were doodles—faces of pretty girls in profile, with piles of hair.

Hanne leafed through the Atlas. In the back she found some drawings, sketched with only a few lines: "Papa Emptying His Pipe." A long-legged man leaning on an umbrella, a large angular face looking near-sightedly up in the air at a bird, one hand emptying the pipe absent-mindedly into the umbrella, which is burning merrily.

Hanne laughed. This must be Miriam's father, gaily drawn. Take that bird—how saucily it gazed at the serious, bespectacled man, who didn't dream that he was on fire. Imagine anyone who could draw her father as funny as that!

She held the next drawing under the lamp: "Agda Sowing Lettuce." A girl bending over, straddling a vegetable bed; a skirt growing tighter over her rear, a little finger standing out stiffly on a hand which is dropping seeds as if they were nuggets of gold. Ten lines in all. Fabulous.

The last drawing read: "Ole Jacob's Latest Sniffle." A little, dark-eyed boy with a big runny nose. A scarf around his neck, blanket over his legs, a "Biggles" book in his hand. Only a few strokes. How wonderful!

Whenever Hanne tried to draw a face or a person, it ended by resembling anything but what she had intended. Arms and legs looked as if they would fall off, everything turned out differently from what she had imagined. She had no control over her own lines and circles, they decided for themselves what they were going to be, and they always decided something stupid.

How different with this unknown girl. With a few strokes she had told a great deal about her family—this must be the eleven year old boy her father had mentioned, and that, the grown sister. But what about Miriam herself? Hanne leafed back and forth in the Atlas and the filled composition books. Not a line about Miriam.

Hanne was sure that Miriam had braids. Why, it wasn't easy to say, but that's how she imagined her. Blonde braids. And when she sat at the desk, she wore a grown-up housecoat as well as small, soft slippers with rabbit fur around the edges, just like the ones Hanne had wanted for Christmas, but hadn't received.

She pushed the books a little to one side on the bookshelf, and put her own beside them. Then she caught sight of the corner of a notebook that had fallen behind the books. She took it out, and on the cover read: "Norwegian Composition, by Miriam Frænkel." Hanne stared at the strange, foreign-sounding name. No, come to think of it, Miriam couldn't have blonde braids. Miriam had to be dark, with brown eyes and short hair. She was Norwegian, at any rate, and made the same mistakes for which Hanne herself had received a minus.

"The First Ski Trip of the Winter." "A Person I Admire." The same compositions as in her own class. She herself had written four-and-a-half pages about the King, and had received "Good," but the composition had not been read aloud because there was a Nazi in the class. Whom had Miriam written about? The poet Wergeland? Strange.

Hanne leafed on. Here was a self-chosen topic: "My Family."

Was she wrong to read these compositions? They *had* been written for a teacher and a whole class. She would never have touched a diary.

"My older sister is called Agda, and she is pretty," Hanne read. "Everyone thinks she is lovely, I do too. Now and then I borrow a dress from her, but when the dress is on me, it stops being lovely. Why, I do not know, for I am not so ugly that I have to spoil a pretty dress. But that's the way it is, at any rate.

"Earlier, Agda was very much the big sister, but now she is engaged, so now she is all right. His name is Georg. Not much of a name, I think. He ought to be called *Per* or *Kare* or *Rolf*. Georg is the kind of name that is given to English kings, not the kind of a name one gets engaged to. He has given me my own perfume, so I don't have to borrow any more from Agda."

This composition is a little childish, thought Hanne, slightly disappointed. She turned back to the cover and looked at the date. Oh well, it was a whole year ago! Not so strange. She went on reading.

"At Christmas I gave him a drawing I made of the view from my window, and he had it framed and hung it on his wall. Agda and Georg are very much in love. When they go for a walk, they lean on each other so hard, that if you took one of them away, the other would fall down.

"Ole Jacob is nine, and looks like a baby bird, says Agda, but she doesn't say it out loud. For he would cry. In the winter he talks through his nose. He is kind—very kind, when he isn't being teased.

"Papa is quite serious. He is a chemist, and his head is so full of formulas and figures that one would think there was no more room for other thoughts, but he always has room to think of us. But I cannot write about Papa. Papa needs a whole composition to himself."

Out of the notebook rose the entire family. Pretty Agda, who stopped being a big sister when she became engaged. Ole Jacob, who resembled a baby bird and had colds all winter. Miriam herself, who was glad she got perfume instead of a little girl thing, who loved her father, and didn't like the name Georg.

What a lovely name, Miriam. If only one had a friend like her, here in this strange city! What fun it would be if she were sitting over in the armchair now, in her housecoat and the slippers with the rabbit fur trim. She herself could sit on the edge of the bed and share her chocolate ration with Miriam.

Hanne pulled off her clothes and kicked the shoes across

the floor. She was tired after the moving, but pretended to be exhausted so as not to have to brush her teeth. Yawning, she turned out the light, pulled up the blackout curtain, and rolled herself into a ball under the covers. Only her head peeped out as she watched the stars in the sky. Almost as many stars now as there were over the cathedral in Trondheim.

Sleep did not come. The house was so new to her, all the sounds so strange. They came from the walls, from the stairs below, as though the rooms were alive. She lay, staring into the darkness, listening to this funny house, where the stairs creaked in the night from the weight of footsteps and people long since gone. And among them was a girl whose name was Miriam. Hanne closed her eyes, and trying to imagine the girl's face, fell asleep.

2. *EVEN THE NICE ONES . . .*

March glided over into a rainy April. Hanne went to her new school and did not think as much about the unknown Miriam, even though she ran into her everywhere in the attic room. A half-finished bit of knitting . . . photographs of girl friends . . . a book, *The Drama of Mayerling,* in which heavy lines had been made in the margins beside all the sad parts. Inside the book was a picture of a boy on skis, and on the back was written "Rolf, my movie friend."

One day, after school, Hanne hopped off the streetcar and sauntered home. The wind was at her back, and the rain drummed on her sou'wester and raincoat. "Headache weather," her mother usually called it, when the wind kept on blowing day in and day out. And even though Hanne, snug in her windblown sou'wester, didn't feel the least trace of a headache, she was still in low spirits. Autumn in the spring is never fun.

A fast-moving truck sent a broad spray of dirty water, which hit the sidewalk with a splash. From a side street she could hear the heelplates of marching German soldiers. This grating sound of metal against the stone was harsh and frightening.

They had made fun of her at school because she spoke differently from the others in the class. It is nauseating to be laughed at when one hasn't said anything funny. Hanne had been talking during lunch period in a Trondheim accent, which was very different from the way people talked in Oslo. Monica, who was the one in the classroom everyone listened to, had asked Hanne what she did with all her "E's." Did she swallow them with her bread? And of course everyone laughed at that. The day before, Monica had been friendly, and the rays of grace had shone on Hanne. The sudden change had been abrupt and bewildering.

She stood still for a moment and looked up the street as the troop of German soldiers swung around the corner and disappeared. Hanne gazed after them absent-mindedly, and thought out a couple of quick retorts to this business of the "E's" and the slice of bread. It helped to think up clever answers. It was almost as though she really had said them, almost as though they had all laughed at Monica.

Ahead lay the factory, huge and expensive looking, produc-
ing Heaven only knew how many pieces of soap in a second.
At the left stood the Laboratory where Dr. Frænkel invented
miracle-working synthetics. Her father, who had been re-
assigned to Oslo from the Trondheim branch, could only
administer these inventions, not make any himself. It didn't
matter much who did what though, since nearly all the
soap was sent to Germany.

Right in front loomed "The Old Court," gray and neg-
lected, standing out from all the newer buildings which
belonged to the factory. The house should have been torn
down long ago, and replaced by a new one with room for
several families instead of just one. But "The Old Court"
still remained, and no one wanted to pay for painting it.
The front of the house resembled an unwashed face between
clean ones, thought Hanne. Strange how the house could be
so pretty inside. She looked up at her own attic window.

"Isn't it nice?" said a voice at her shoulder.

Hanne whirled around. A girl stood beside her. She was
Hanne's height and wore a raincoat and sou'wester like
Hanne's.

"Aren't you Hanne . . . Hoygard?" asked the girl, hesi-
tating, as if she wasn't certain whether she remembered the
name correctly.

Hanne knew right away that the girl was Miriam, even
though the face was not what she had imagined. The eyes
were not brown but gray, and they were long and narrow,
under straight brows.

"Oh! It's Miriam!" The words burst out of Hanne. She

reached out her hand and took Miriam by the arm as if she were afraid that this girl, who had suddenly turned up, would dissolve in smoke and disappear again.

"How could you know that?"

"Only guessed. I've been thinking a lot about you. Why, I live in your room."

"Do you suppose I could come up for a moment? I'd like so much to pick up some things."

"Of course you can."

"Then we'll go by the kitchen stairs." Miriam at once took the lead. Instead of going in the front door, she went, at home, around to the back door which she opened with her own key. Without looking into the kitchen, where Mrs. Hoygard was busy with pots and pans, the girls sneaked past, as if by mutual agreement, silently up the stairs to the attic.

"Be careful, there's a step here that creaks," said Miriam.

It was a little strange to be shown the way in her own home by a girl she had never laid eyes on before. But, as it began that day, so it continued throughout their entire friendship. Miriam took the lead, Hanne followed.

The girls pulled off their wet things and hung them over the railing at the top of the stairs. Miriam had on a turtlenecked sweater. With her slight figure, dark hair, thick brows over gray eyes, she was a decided contrast to Hanne's blonde robustness. She had a graceful neck and her hair fell in waves that seemed wild and gay around the calm face, as though she had just walked out of a whirlwind.

What a lovely smile she has, thought Hanne. She admired

Miriam precisely because she was so different from herself.

Miriam stood in the middle of the floor sniffing at the air in the room. "Why do old houses smell so much better than new ones?" she asked.

"Have you moved into a new house?" Hanne thought with astonishment of all the furniture the Frænkels had left behind.

"No, we're living with friends of Papa's." Miriam went over and moved a vase a little, straightened a book. Hanne could tell how much Miriam missed all the things she went about touching. Hanne felt a little ill at ease, as if she were an intruder.

"Miriam, I'm sorry about this. Sorry I've taken your room!"

"Are you crazy? Your parents are being more than kind."

Hanne knew that Dr. Frænkel was at the factory now and then. No one knew when he came or left. Papa said he was indispensable at the laboratory.

"Kind of you to hang onto all our old furniture. Papa says it may save our home."

They were talking of things now which were better left unspoken. Hanne said that what they were doing was just nice, and there was a slight pause. *Nice* was such a stupid word for this bad time.

Hanne lifted the curtain with the picture of Cary Grant on it. "Do you like him?"

"That was mostly last year. This year I like Tyrone Power."

"Oh, no! Cary's much nicer."

For a while they discussed Cary's pros and cons. The rain

drummed against the window, heavy and gray, like a curtain that shut out the light, and made the whole room half dark.

"My window is the only one in the house that has a view," said Miriam. "I mean *your* window is the only one that has a view," she added hastily.

"Oh stop! It's *yours*. Once this stupid war is over, and the Germans beaten, it'll be yours again. Maybe by fall. By Christmas, at any rate."

Hanne didn't ask Miriam *why* she had had to leave her lovely room. Hanne had learned like everybody else in occupied countries that a single phrase, a hint of an address, might put the Gestapo on the trail. So it was wise not to say anything *anywhere*. But since it was the war, and only the war, which made decent people hide away—for reasons not mentioned and not questioned—why, as soon as the war was over all those tucked-away people would creep out of their hiding places and go back to their homes again. Probably by fall or by Christmas.

"Well, yes." Miriam thought so too. A wâr which came so suddenly and unexpectedly, had to end as suddenly and unexpectedly.

They stood looking down at the river, the air between them full of confidence in spite of unspoken questions and answers. The storm had free play, and the force of the wind could be felt against the wall which creaked. Miriam sat down on the windowseat.

"Have you ever heard so many sounds as there are up here? Are you afraid to be alone in this room?"

"A little bit. But I'd rather be afraid up here than safe downstairs. It's so nice."

"I think so too. Papa used to sleep in the room below. We had a system of signals. When I knocked two times, it meant: 'Goodnight! Sleep tight!' And when I knocked three times, it meant: 'I've been dreaming! Come up!' And then he came right away."

"You must have a kind Papa."

"Very kind."

"My father says they can't do without him at the Laboratory."

"They may have to." Miriam sighed.

Pause.

"Can't you come and visit me now and then? I'm new here in town, haven't any friends yet."

Miriam smiled at her. She took the key for the back door from her pocket and put it on the table.

"I won't be allowed to come. But thanks just the same."

"Are you here without permission?"

"I'm here without permission."

"What did you want to get?"

"Oh, not very much. My rubber boots. But most of all I came because I *had* to come back once."

Hanne found the rubber boots in the back of the closet. There were holes in them, but they could probably be vulcanized. Suddenly she realized that Miriam's shoes were soaking wet.

"Sit down here!" She shoved the little armchair closer to

the heater. "You can't go like that." She pulled off Miriam's shoes and stockings, and slipped her own slippers on Miriam's feet. Now it was the way she had day-dreamed in the beginning. Miriam sat in the armchair, while she, Hanne, sat on the edge of the bed. Only the ration of chocolate was missing. But Hanne had eaten it.

"Do you have slippers with rabbit fur edges?"

"Me? No. Why?"

"They seemed to go so well with you and—" Hanne motioned with her hand, "the whole room."

"Do rabbit fur edges go with the room?"

"Yes, don't you think so?"

Miriam laughed. It was the first time Hanne had heard her laugh.

"You're funny. But I like you. It's nice that someone I like is living in my room."

So! Miriam liked her. That slim, pretty girl sitting there wearing her slippers liked her! Maybe Miriam was a little Oslo-smart and sure of herself. But not the way Monica was. Monica, who looked people up and down until the clothes seemed to shrink on their bodies, and it seemed every garment one owned was stupid and outgrown, even the newest pair of slacks. But Miriam wasn't like Monica. Miriam was sweet.

Lacking the chocolate ration, Hanne handed Miriam a box of cough drops, and the girls sucked on them while the stockings dried.

"I know more about you than you think. I read your composition. Are you angry?"

"Composition? Which composition?"

"The one about your family, of course."

"Oh that! No indeed, not in the least."

"And I also saw all your pencil marks in the *Mayerling*."

"Oh. Yes, I read it last year. Then I was so romantic."

"I've read it now. It's super. I cried a long time."

They sat quietly, busy with the licorice drops.

"Tell me a little more about your family. Your mother?" Hanne spoke again.

"She died years and years ago."

"Oh." Hanne had noticed that she was not in the composition, but thought Miriam had grown tired after writing about her brother and sister. It had not occurred to Hanne that anyone as matter-of-course as a mother would not be alive.

"I was only five when she died. Once in a while I remember her face. She used to tuck the quilt around, making me snug and warm. There wasn't a draft on my back the way there is when Papa tucks me in now."

"Does your father really empty his pipe into the umbrella?"

Miriam laughed and her eyes turned into two twinkling stripes that were fun to watch.

"He did one day when he was especially absent-minded. He's always thinking of so many things. The umbrella burned up."

"Are Agda and Georg still just as much in love?"

"Are they? You should see Georg. Whenever Agda does something or other that's really typical, something only she does—that quick little jerk of her head to get her hair out of her eyes, for example, or the funny way she takes hold of her elbows—he stands still and smiles, and looks at her as if it were a long time since he had last seen her. And yesterday at dinner, when Papa handed him the soup, Georg stuck his whole hand in it just because Agda happened to be talking on the telephone behind him, and he had to look at her. You and I could certainly be in love, too, but we wouldn't stick our hands in the soup because of it."

No, Hanne had never stuck her hand in the soup. Three times she had been in love—twice, very much; once, only a little.

"Tell me something about *your* family now," said Miriam.

Hanne stopped to think. After all, what was there to tell about her kind, housewifely mother, who stood in lines for them, and made large portions out of small rations? Or about her plump, kind, home-loving father, whose joy was to go bicycling in Orland, and always knew when Hanne was unhappy? She didn't have brothers and sisters who were in love, or had colds, or did funny things.

"You don't have a mother, and I don't have brothers and sisters," Hanne said. It was as though they had something in common that way. "We're a pretty ordinary family, but I think you'll like us," she added. "Where did you learn to draw so well?"

"Nowhere. When I've finished school, I'm going to try to enter the Art Academy. What do you like to do?"

Again Hanne had to stop and think. What did she like to do? What could she do?

"Nothing much. Except knit mittens. And go skiing."

"Not at the same time, of course?"

"No, I don't usually knit with skis on."

They laughed over this. Hanne was having even more fun than she had dreamed of.

"What a nice sweater you have." Miriam leaned forward and felt the sleeve. "Thick enough, and a lovely color. I've been looking for something like it."

"It's quite inexpensive," said Hanne, flattered. "I bought it in Trondheim. In a Jew-store."

There was a pause then, and to fill it in—for their friendship was still too new to stand pauses—she added, "We have so many Jew-stores in Trondheim. You know, the cheap kind with gaudy colors and low prices. But you can find nice things now and then."

Miriam still did not reply, only turned red, and the flush spread all the way up under the roots of her hair at the temples. And suddenly the truth struck Hanne. Miriam, herself, was a Jew! Why hadn't she thought of it before? That was why the Frænkels were in hiding. Everything fit —the unusual name, the dark hair, the essay on Wergeland who had been the benefactor of the Jews in Norway—everything fit. Miriam and her family were Jews.

Hanne shut her eyes. In one burning second she saw before her the humiliations, the atrocities committed by the Nazis against Jewish Norwegians who, until then, had lived peacefully in the country without anyone thinking of them as being different from anybody else.

And now she had hurt her new friend. Said silly things

about cheap and gaudy Jew-stores. Hanne was no better than Hitler himself, she thought. Why did she always have to pop out with stupid things? It seemed to her that the words she had just uttered flashed in letters of fire in the air. And this friendship had looked so promising only a moment ago. Unhappily she stretched out her hand and touched Miriam's elbow.

"I didn't know. . . . " she stammered. "I didn't mean. . . ."

Miriam hadn't said a single word, just sat looking out the window, a little tired, as though she were accustomed to hearing that sort of thing. At last she turned and smiled comfortingly into Hanne's unhappy eyes.

"Don't let it bother you," she said. "Even the nice ones say things like that. Just don't let it bother you."

3 SQUEEZED-IN BIRTHDAY

Miriam's sixteenth birthday dawned in two rooms in a west-side villa. Large and small packages were piled on the breakfast table. Outside the windows the sky was clearing.

Miriam had dreaded the day, she knew exactly how it would be. Papa would put on an act, and pretend he was happy and in good spirits. Everyone would put on an act; she, too, would pretend that this was the happiest of all birthdays.

In reality they had been pretending ever since they had moved here.

Papa would smile at her admiringly and say, "You're looking more and more like your mother." For he said it every
birthday. And later, the two dreadful boys on the first floor
would come running headlong up and stamp about, follow
each bite of food with their eyes, shout, roar, question,
question! And their mother, who was only too happy to
have a free moment, would not call them down again. And
Miriam and her family were so grateful for the chance to
live with these kind people that they would not ask the twins
to leave.

Her family had not yet seated themselves at the table
when she came in, but stood waiting for Miriam. They had
gotten up early. A birthday breakfast was no hasty affair
here in this house. Dr. Frænkel rubbed his hands to make
them warm. It was a cold spring, and one couldn't turn on
the heat in April. Ole Jacob, who had caught a new cold
before he was through with the old one, had a scarf tied
around his throat. Only Agda looked as though she got
along just as well in this uncomfortable· house as she had
back home in "The Old Court." But then Agda had enough
with herself and her own joys; nothing could rob her of her
good humor. No, Agda did not need to pretend. She rolled
up the wide sleeves of her housecoat and arranged things
on the breakfast table, lit candles. Then she flung her hair
up from her forehead with a toss of her head, and gave
Miriam a kiss.

"Happy Birthday! Why, even I think you've grown a
little since last night."

"Gooooood morning and Happy Birthday!" Papa's voice

was full of birthday. "More and more like your mother!"
She went over and received a kiss on her forehead. That big,
angular, kind face of his—how he struggled to keep it cheerful to match the day! He winked one eye behind his glasses,
and patted her on the back. "I do believe you're going to be
just as pretty too, in time. You can be glad that you resemble
your mother, my dear!"

She couldn't very well contradict him. The family sat
down at the table, and Miriam saw how hard they had tried
to make everything as home-like as possible. Many candles
were burning, despite the fact that it was April-bright outside, and this little room was not as pleasant with candles
as the big, gloomy dining room in "The Old Court." The
curtains were drawn—to hide the view of the large white
neighboring villa—and the little veranda table had been
festively covered with a much-too-long cloth, which hung
down onto the floor. A poor but well-meant resemblance
to better birthdays.

Ole Jacob sat with an expectant face above the woolen
scarf. His present was lying outermost to the left, and his
eyes never left it.

Miriam opened the package on top—letter paper in a light
blue box from Papa. Last year she had also received letter
paper, but with her name and address in the corner. This
time the name and address had been left off.

"A thousand thanks, Papa! How pretty!" So like impractical Papa to give her letter paper when she had no one to
write to.

She noticed how Ole Jacob's eyes were glued to the little

package on the left, so she picked it up next. It was an egg-cup, a highly complicated egg-cup in the shape of a rabbit, who, with a polite expression, held out half a china eggshell to the birthday child. The body was hollow, to put salt into, the head full of holes. It sat on so loosely that, when the egg-cup was being initiated, the top fell off, sending cascades of salt over Miriam's unfortunate egg. It had cost Ole Jacob much toil and many doubts to buy this present. It had been exciting to see if there would be enough money, to guess if Miriam would like it (sisters think many pretty things are ugly), or if he could hide it in their tight quarters where there were few hiding places. And most important, if anyone would make fun of it. He was a little taken aback when the head fell off, but the accident was lost in Miriam's expressions of gratitude and praise.

After the egg had been eaten under general observation, Miriam opened another package. Lime-green woolen material from Papa. A new dress, in itself, was a sensation in times like these, and this beautiful fabric was a very special sensation.

"Miss Lepsoe has promised to sew it," said Agda. "You must go there today."

"Tomorrow," said Miriam. She wanted to have the dress made, but Miss Lepsoe was a bit of a trial. She had a habit of finding deficiencies and figure faults in her customers. No, Miriam didn't want to go to Miss Lepsoe today.

Miriam draped the material around her slender hips, and then had to go over and admire herself in the mirror. "How lovely, Papa! A thousand, thousand thanks!" Now she knew what she would do. She would ask Hanne to go to Miss Lepsoe's with her. If Agda went along, she and Miss Lepsoe would decide the cut between them, right over Miriam's head.

The next package was a home-made pullover from Agda. Miriam had caught glimpses of it everywhere for the past three months, and had pretended not to see it.

"It's lovely, Agda. Thanks so much. You *are* an angel. And as busy as you are with your trousseau and everything."

"You *know* I'm an angel," said Agda, accustomed to praise and admiration for everything she undertook. "Pullovers like that really take ever so long. And what a job it is to find any yarn at all."

"Can't you knit one for me too?" begged Ole Jacob. "Gray, with green borders."

"Oh, you want one just like Arnt's," laughed Agda. "No! I'm not copying that loud-mouthed boy. You can keep him!"

Ole Jacob looked hurt. His new friend, Arnt Andresen, was not popular in the family, and in a way Ole Jacob understood why. One never knew what Arnt would say, or what he would do. But, for that very reason, he was so exciting.

Scarcely had Miriam pulled the sweater over her head when Agda jumped up at the ringing of a bicycle bell outside. Forgotten were both Miriam and the sweater.

"Georg! It must be Georg! How sweet of him to drop by to congratulate you," Agda said and rushed out on the balcony, leaving the door open. "Hurry and come up!" she called down to him.

Miriam was not quite so touched. She knew only too

well that Georg used every excuse to catch a glimpse of Agda—and it was cold with the door open.

Miriam poured the coffee, wearing her new sweater, which looked as though it had been made to grow in, while Agda went down to meet Georg . . . and sure enough, was gone for an eternity.

There they came at last, Georg with bicycle guards around his ankles, and a bouquet in his hand.

"Many happy returns, Miriam! How wonderful you look today." He handed her the flowers with a bow. "If you keep on like that, you'll end up being another Agda!"

Miriam kissed him on the cheek, enchanted by the flowers, less enchanted by the compliment. Strange that one always had to resemble someone else in order to be pretty.

She placed the flowers on the over-crowded table. Georg sat close to Agda.

Miriam opened still another present. Wergeland's Poems in a new edition, from Papa. He had put one package after the other on the table in an attempt to make the day as *normal* as possible. She knew him well enough.

"Thanks, oh thanks a million!" Miriam tried to vary her expressions of gratitude, but to do so was difficult. She pulled Papa's large head down to her own and kissed him on the forehead, went back and leafed through the book, and read a few lines from the poem "The Jew."

For the Frænkel family was a well-brought-up family. The children had learned to linger over each package, not to race through the pile with short, hasty thanks to right and left.

"A new Wergeland may come to the world at any moment," said Ole Jacob to no one in particular. A new Wergeland would be a consolation to the world in general, not only to the Jews.

"Just now I think he is quite far away," said the more sober Agda.

"They say that Goebbels is coming to Oslo to organize the persecution of the Jews," said Georg.

"Fie, Georg!" Agda turned towards him as though he were the one who had evil plans against the Jews. "How *can* you say such a thing at a birthday table?"

"You're right. Always right." He took her hand and kissed it. "Excuse me, Miriam."

Dr. Frænkel sighed, but it was the first sigh that day.

But now Ole Jacob began to be a little impatient.

"Aren't we going to taste the cake? Otherwise 'The Katzenjammer Kids' will just come and devour everything."

Hardly were the words out of his mouth before they heard tramping and shouting on the stairs. The door to the cold hallway was thrown wide open, and their two tormentors, the twins on the first floor, tumbled, cheerful and in high spirits, into the room. They had rosy cheeks and strong lungs.

"See there, now begins a new course in self-control," said Agda. She took a firm grip on both elbows, as if to hold herself together in the midst of the whirlwind.

"Quick, Georg! Come here and get a piece of cake. Best to take it while you can . . ."

She started to cut the cake but was startled by something up against the window, and dropped the knife on the floor.

"Ugh! What in all the world is that?"

They all turned and saw a face pressed against the pane, so hard that nose and all other features ran together into a pink blob, and only the hair and eyes were recognizable.

Georg got up and took a couple of angry steps towards the balcony door. Then the face drew back, became a real face with nose and mouth, a laughing boyish mouth full of white teeth.

"Arnt!" Agda exclaimed. Arnt, Ole Jacob's adored and formidable friend. No one else would think of climbing up to the second story just to scare the Frænkels.

"Well, he can just climb down again . . ." said Agda, furiously. "Don't let him in!"

Her heart was still pounding. The mask on the window-pane had been so terrifying, completely resembling a crushed face with living eyes.

"But he hasn't done anything wrong," said Ole Jacob. "Just wanted to frighten us a little. The way you carry on about nothing!"

"Invite him in and give him a piece of cake," said Dr. Frænkel. "Then perhaps he will use the stairs the next time."

Arnt always made them disagree a little.

4 *MISS LEPSOE*

The friendship between Miriam and Hanne blossomed quickly that spring. It was as though the attic room were a bond between them, as though they owned something together. Miriam soon yielded to the temptation to come back, no matter how forbidden it might be.

"Ohhhhhhh!" she said, stretching her arms wide as soon as she was inside the door. "You ought to know what it's like to write a composition with the twins climbing up your back and breathing down your neck. How nice and quiet it is here!"

No homeless bedding here, no dirty cups to be washed in an enamel basin with wide edges, only to become dirty again. Here all was lovely.

On Sundays the girls took trips on their bicycles with Miriam's "movie friend," Rolf. He was the tallest boy Hanne had ever seen. He grew so fast that he got headaches. But he had a handsome face, and, so as not to fall in love with him, Hanne had fallen in love as quickly as possible with his friend Terje.

Terje was a challenge. The very first time they were together, he had said, "Girls who have no interests, you can keep!"

Hanne became terrified, and the whole week she racked her brain for "interests." At last she decided to become interested in butterflies. In the first place, they were pretty, and in the second place, they had difficult and strange names: "Red-spotted Apollo," "Night Peacock's Eye," "Blue Admiral." Nothing impressed Terje so much as names and expressions that signified knowledge. She read an article about Lemon Butterflies and Moths, and went into a bookstore to buy a book with more names. But, when she heard the price —24 kroner—she abandoned the interest entirely. And no more Blue Admirals or Red-spotted Apollos fluttered in and out of Hanne's conversation the next Sunday.

Terje intended to study astronomy as soon as he entered the University, he said, and Hanne, who loved the starry skies, became excited at once. Until she discovered that it wasn't the stars that were the most important, but physics and figures. Endless amounts of figures.

But Terje was good looking, and nice in his way. And *of course* she was in love with him.

She listened to him when he rattled on about light years and planetary shifting. Strange how unpoetic stars became when Terje started talking about them.

"Ten million light years," said Terje. And Hanne, who couldn't help being more romantic than Terje, thought how nice it would be if sweethearts could love one another for ten million light years.

When Miriam invited Hanne to go to the seamstress, Hanne asked if she could take along a piece of flowered dress material for herself, about which she was uncertain. Miriam did not object. She liked to help when Hanne was uncertain, liked to lead. Rolf and Terje accompanied the girls and the four of them walked for a while in Stens Park, where the gardeners had started working in the flower beds. Rolf and Miriam kept ahead. It was one of those days when Rolf had a headache from growing so much. Nonetheless, the two talked the whole time, and Hanne, who followed with a taciturn Terje, couldn't believe that there was so much to talk about in the world. The same week she had bought a book about beetles for three kroner and fifty ore, and now, she searched for beetles with strange names to dazzle Terje. That day he had just gotten a new bicycle, which he wheeled alongside as they sauntered. With a new bicycle he seemed even more conceited than usual.

It was cloudy, and a mild, southerly breeze was blowing over the city. It had called at many places, and brought with it that good, strange smell of earth which accompanies the first unscented flowers of spring. Hanne strolled along the soggy lawn, and over to a spaded-up bed, while voicing her opinion as to which movie they ought to see after the fitting. She found no beetles, but just as they were leaving the park, she came across a golden brown, flannel-like caterpillar, which she picked up in her hand. She couldn't really identify it, but she could always make believe.

"What's that you're swooning over this time?" said Terje. He wasn't half as polite as Rolf.

Hanne pretended not to hear, just studied the caterpillar with an expert expression on her face. "Do you know what this kind of caterpillar moves on, Terje?"

"Caterpillar feet, of course!" Terje was seldom in doubt about anything.

"Wrong!"

"Suction cups, then?"

"Wrong again!"

"Walking warts?"

"No, silly!" Hanne turned the caterpillar back on its stomach. "Abdominal prolegs!"

They were just about to jaywalk across the street. Hanne had stopped for a car and did not notice that Terje was already across, missing her lesson in natural science altogether, and she fired the crazy words right into the ear of an elderly gentleman. He looked at her gravely, as if he were thinking: "Young ladies did not talk that way to gentlemen in my day!"

Hanne blushed, and then she became angry. Terje was

an idiot! What kind of manners were those to run from her without letting her finish what she was saying!

"Why did you run away in the middle of what I was telling you?" She caught up with him on the other sidewalk, where he stood waiting. "Here I stand making a fool of myself."

"I didn't run, I heard very well what you said. But why are you wasting time with those wretched prolegs of yours?"

"You're making fun of me! You're nasty! Now I'm going to take this poor little caterpillar back to the park! Goodbye!" She turned away from him.

"Hanne! Wait!" He flung down the bicycle, and was after her, took her wrist and shook the caterpillar into his hand. "*I'll* do it. To think that you could be so angry!" He disappeared through the passageway.

"Preferably on a bush!" shouted Hanne after him.

"Preferably on a bush!" echoed back from the passageway.

Hanne was in a more reconciliatory mood. His friendship was rough, no doubt, but he *was* nice in his way, hadn't forgotten that she hated to put beetles and caterpillars down on an asphalt street.

Miss Lepsoe lived all the way up in Theresegate. Rolf and Terje went to the doorway of the tall, gray apartment house with them. They agreed to meet out in front of the movies later that evening. After the German short-subject, of course, which was pure propaganda and wouldn't be seen by any decent Norwegian.

Miss Lepsoe received the girls in the dining room, which

was her fitting-room and sewing-room. Bulky furniture forced them to squeeze past sideways. Over the dining room table, which was overflowing with pieces of cloth and fashion magazines, hung a red lampshade with long flounces. Miss Lepsoe had raised it on one side, so that half the room lay in a reddish twilight, while the other half was glaringly lighted by a 100-watt bulb that blinded the eyes. Miriam had never seen the room any other way. Miss Lepsoe tried to combat the gloomy yard outside with a bright light and a romantic lampshade. Brown curtains hung in front of the only window. A radio—to which Miss Lepsoe's ears had long since been deaf—blared raucously all the while they were there.

"I've brought along a friend who would like to have a flowered summer dress made," said Miriam. "Can you take her too?"

"I suppose I'll have to." Miss Lepsoe fingered the material. "But she should have picked material that was more slimming."

The girls hung over the table and leafed through the fashion magazines. Miriam soon knew what she wanted, but Hanne couldn't decide. All the dresses were pretty on the slender-waisted beauties, but she knew, of course, that the most tempting fashions might be difficult for her to wear.

"I had thought of something like this." She looked up questioningly into Miss Lepsoe's stern eyes. They expressed no enthusiasm.

"You're too short-waisted for that." Miss Lepsoe quickly leafed to the back where children and little girls romped over the pages.

Children's styles! Hanne was hurt. But at the same time she became uncertain and confused, for hadn't Miriam said that Miss Lepsoe was clever at dressing the customers according to their *types?*

Miriam intervened. "I think you should take a tailored cut," she said, and the words alone were enough to draw Hanne out of the nursery where Miss Lepsoe had placed her. Miriam turned to the front of the magazine, and pointed to a young lady stepping out of a limousine, certain of conquest.

"Well, she'll need pleats across the chest then," said Miss Lepsoe severely, "or else she'll be too flat!" She had a mania for discovering figure faults, which could be hidden by cut, and tricks and sewing skill. But Hanne was enraptured because Miriam had decided that her type stepped out of a limousine, surrounded by young men, rather than skipped rope on the last page of the magazine.

The radio was broadcasting the weather forecast. How like Miss Lepsoe to have her radio tuned to Oslo, when everyone else was now listening to London. But she didn't hear a word of what was being said. She had just gotten into the habit of having the noise in the room.

Miriam draped the material over her shoulder while Miss Lepsoe took measurements. Dreamily, Miriam looked into the mirror where she saw herself, wrapped in lime-green wool, between the oak dining room chairs. A new dress always filled her with excitement, as though it would surely make her prettier than any dress she had ever owned before. Great things would be experienced in it. A new dress was a small part of the future.

The radio was now broadcasting the news: A stream of German victories and Allied defeats. Miss Lepsoe heard neither, and Miriam stood deep in thought. She didn't realize that the announcer was talking about Goebbels, who was going to pay Oslo a visit.

Every child knew who Goebbels was. Every child knew that a visit by him would bring no good. Somehow or other the news must suddenly have penetrated Miss Lepsoe's radio-deafened ears, for she burst out:

"Goebbels! That nasty Jew! If only he were sitting in Palestine!"

Miss Lepsoe was a good, patriotic Norwegian, and she railed at Goebbels with the first and worst oath she could think of. It struck Miriam like a whiplash.

"Jew?" she said slowly. "Why he persecutes the Jews. He can't very well be a Jew then!"

"No?" said Miss Lepsoe absent-mindedly. "Well, he looks like one, at any rate!"

Hanne, rising halfway up out of her chair, cried out: "If he were a Jew, he would have more sense!" As always, whenever she became angry, she started talking with a thick Trondheim accent.

Undisturbed, Miss Lepsoe went on taking Miriam's measurements. She was no more aware of their distress than she was of the victories and defeats announced on the radio.

"Well, he's a villain at any rate. They say he wants to take our radios away from us and put everybody in jail. We'll make the collar a little high, so your neck won't be too long. I never saw a back this small!" She wrote down figures in a notebook. "Well, I'll make the summer dress first. There's not such a hurry with a woolen dress now that it's spring."

She accompanied the two silent girls through the kitchen to the front door, which she opened to a hall smelling of fried fish.

"Goodbye, goodbye. Don't come back until I tell you to."

They were out on the street again. Miriam walked with her head bowed. She wanted so much to say something clever and funny about Miss Lepsoe, who used the word "Jew" as a swear word, but she couldn't manage it. She was a little nauseous from the lack of ventilation in the stuffy fitting room.

It had rained and now the air was as cold and clear as a mountain stream. She filled her lungs. How terrible it must be to work, day in and day out, in such a closed-in room, looking out on a gloomy backyard. A backyard where bad smells from old dinners always lingered. Everything considered, Miss Lepsoe was probably a little pathetic. Look how she tried to make things nice with that awful red lampshade, and had no more sense than to think that Goebbels was a Jew! Miriam walked up Theresegate and forgave Miss Lepsoe.

"Thanks for saying that Goebbels would have more sense if he were a Jew." Miriam suddenly had to laugh at Hanne's outburst. But immediately afterwards she sighed. Hanne, who wasn't a Jew herself, could say things like that.

Hanne brightened when she saw Miriam laugh. She had been walking on pins, not knowing which was worse—to speak or keep silent. She had decided to keep quiet, but wondered if it wouldn't have been better to divert Miriam by talking. Only Hanne didn't quite know what to say.

"Oh Miriam, I could have murdered that stupid woman!"

"Poor thing. She didn't even know I was a Jew. But what I find so strange is that people can be so angry at the Jews when they know so little about them. How many do you think Miss Lepsoe knows? One? Two?"

"None," said Hanne with conviction. She squeezed Miriam's arm under hers. "That's just why, of course."

"There *are* unpleasant Jews too," Miriam said sincerely.

"Well, there certainly are unpleasant Norwegians too. But no one says they're unpleasant *because* they're Norwegian!"

Arm in arm they walked up the street, talking about everything but Goebbels and Miss Lepsoe. Hanne didn't fall back into her Trondheim accent except when she was upset. She practiced and practiced every day, so that no one would make fun of her at school. For it is a strange thing in this world that if anyone stands out a little, whether it is because of his accent, or race or religion, he is tormented by all the others who resemble one another. This both girls had both been made to feel.

Suddenly they started running after a bus. They remembered that it was getting late, and Rolf and Terje were waiting for them outside the movies.

5 DANGEROUS ASSIGNMENT

Anyone who has not lived in an occupied country will find it difficult to imagine what conditions are like, or understand the strain that lies on everyone, adults and children alike. The daily strain of anxiety and caution. On the streets in Norway, words were whispered more than spoken, usually accompanied by a quick glance over the shoulder to make sure inquisitive ears were not in the vicinity to hear what was being said. Illegal newspapers, written in attics and closets, went their hidden rounds from hand to hand, and the school children were eager messengers.

When it was rumored that Goebbels was coming to Oslo tempers flared. Ole Jacob knew that in Rolf's and Terje's class there were plans afoot, dangerous plans, for Rolf had talked with Miriam about them, while he was taking her bicycle apart and putting it together again. The eleventh grade of Katedral School was going to show Goebbels how little they thought of him.

Ole Jacob sat beside Rolf, who was black to the elbows from bicycle grease, and helped him with the hub. It wasn't the first time Ole Jacob had been initiated into secret plans. Last summer he and Rolf had put out an illegal newspaper, which they had called "Norway's Voice." The name had been Ole Jacob's idea, and he had been asked to collaborate with the big boys because he owned a typewriter. Old and worn to be sure, but a treasure all the same, and ever since the day he had gotten it and carried it triumphantly up to his room in "The Old Court," the house had echoed with the sound of Ole Jacob clattering on the keys. One day, when Rolf had accompanied Miriam home from a movie and heard the typing exercises from the second floor, he had offered his partnership. Ole Jacob was in seventh heaven. The edition was small on Ole Jacob's ramshackle machine, and they would distribute only 18 copies at a time. The sheets, full of small mistakes and big news, were dropped into unsuspecting mailboxes in the neighborhood. Only when the typewriter broke down and needed repairs which exceeded their powers, only then was "Norway's Voice" silenced.

But now it was a question of more dangerous ventures than schoolboy newspapers.

"Rolf," said Ole Jacob, "can't I come in on this?"

"You know you can't," said Rolf, taking the monkey wrench Miriam handed to him, "and if you breathe a word about it, we're not friends any more."

"What do you take me for?"

Rolf concentrated on a stubborn nut he was tightening.

"No. All right, then we won't say any more about it. Hand me that cotton waste, please."

The dirtier and oilier Rolf became, the brighter Miriam's bicycle shone. But Ole Jacob wiped his own fingers carefully on a wad of cotton waste, and lifted his bicycle up from the gravel driveway. It wasn't so much that he couldn't take part that mattered—that was even bearable—but it was the way Rolf refused that was so awful. As if Ole Jacob was a little runny-nosed boy, someone to be mostly ignored. There certainly wasn't anybody here who would miss him, so he left.

Out in the street a swarm of boys bicycled in curves and loops. First they came by, flocklike, sweeping around a corner with one foot on the ground, then they dismounted and stood in a group, shouting to one another. Jingling bells and shrill boyish voices filled the air. In a gateway, an illegal newspaper was circulating. Here they whispered instead of shouted, and there was a conspicuous silence around the dirty scrap of paper.

Arnt Andresen, the boy who had interrupted Miriam's

birthday breakfast, stood reading the paper. There was something about Arnt that Ole Jacob both feared and admired. One never knew how to take him. His eyes were pale, slightly red-rimmed, almost without lashes, and to Ole Jacob there seemed to be something cruel about them. Once he had seen Arnt torture a frog. Ole Jacob wasn't particularly squeamish, but the sight of that frog which Arnt kept tormenting had made him furious. Yet at times Arnt was kind. One day, early in the spring, he had plunged through the ice on Frogner Pond to rescue a duck that had frozen fast. Trouble was . . . one never knew whether he was in a rescuing or tormenting mood.

"Let me see!" Ole Jacob reached out his hand. He spoke abruptly for he was upset by Rolf's seeming indifference to him.

The scrap of paper had been in and out of so many back pockets that only a dirty tatter was left. It looked as if it had been read to pieces. Arnt handed it past Ole Jacob to another boy, a tow-headed, freckled eleven-year-old named Emil.

"It's not anything for you! You're not Norwegian!"

"I'm not Norwegian?" Ole Jacob was more astonished than angry. He almost had to laugh. "I'm not Norwegian?" he repeated.

Arnt fixed his strange eyes on Ole Jacob. "Of course you're not! Just go and look at yourself in the mirror!"

One or two boys in the crowd snickered. There is always someone who has to snicker when smart-alecky things are said. Ole Jacob happened to be standing between Emil and another tow-headed boy with a turned-up nose, and undoubtedly Ole Jacob, with his dark eyes and long, narrow nose, did stand out and look different. Some of the boys stared at him searchingly, as if they had suddenly noticed him for the first time. Until then, they had all bicycled, and talked and fought together in boyish friendliness. Now it was as though they had begun to see him with new eyes.

"Just look at that nose," Arnt went on.

"He must be half-Norwegian, at any rate," Emil said quietly. It was meant as a kind of defense.

Ole Jacob turned on him angrily. For one reason or another these words seemed even more insulting than those of Arnt. Half-Norwegian—that was almost the same as half-witted. The blood rushed to his cheeks, reached his forehead; it was like a burning fuse nearing dynamite. Speechless, with furious eyes, he attacked the one boy he had considered his best friend on the block. Emil, who hadn't for a moment expected such an attack, didn't have a chance to put up his guard, before he was lying on the sidewalk. Ole Jacob hit and hammered away at a face which tried to wriggle aside, kept on hitting until the sight of blood brought him to his senses. Only then did the thought strike him that he should have hit someone else—certainly not his friend.

He got up, panting. Rolf rode by on Miriam's bicycle, giving it a trial spin. Over the ring of on-lookers he caught sight of Ole Jacob but did not recognize him at first. This boy, usually so peaceful, had changed. It suddenly occurred to Rolf that this was how a madman must look. Then Rolf realized the boy was Miriam's brother. He jumped off the bicycle.

"What's going on here?"

Silence.

Emil stood crying. Blood and tears ran into a dirty handkerchief.

"I . . . I only said he was half-Norwegian . . . I didn't mean . . ."

Arnt's teasing laughter could be heard behind the ring of boys.

"Ha! Ha! He's not half-Norwegian, he's whole Jew!" Some of the boys snickered.

Rolf dropped the bicycle in a flash, was over Arnt before he could catch his breath.

"And you . . ." Rolf shook him. "You don't talk like a Norwegian, you talk like a Nazi!" He spit out his chewing gum onto the sidewalk as if to show his disgust. "Worse than Goebbels himself!"

In a second the mood of the on-lookers changed. Rolf, broad-shouldered and as straight as a tree in a forest, towered over Arnt, then gave him one last shake before he let him go.

"You haven't thought of being a Nazi, eh? That's the way you're carrying on!"

"Let me go!" cried Arnt, without realizing that he was already free. "Just because you run to the movies with his sister, you . . ."

This time there was no one who laughed, no one who

looked up to him. A higher verdict had declared that only Nazis talked such arrogant nonsense.

Emil, who was the innocent cause of the commotion, stood confused, a little afraid that Rolf's fury would turn on him. He blew his nose. But Rolf paid no attention to him. He took Ole Jacob by the arm, almost the way a policeman arrests a drunk. And Ole Jacob did look dizzy, too, standing there reeling after the violent fight.

"Listen here, Frænkel," said Rolf, using the last name to give weight to his words. "I need a reliable fellow tomorrow afternoon. Was just looking for you."

Tomorrow afternoon, why that was when Goebbels was coming.

"A . . . real, patriotic Norwegian, that is."

"Aye, aye," said Ole Jacob weakly. Rolf went off with him, and Ole Jacob felt as if he were dangling happily in the strong fist that had lifted him from the depths of despair straight up to the skies.

* * * * *

Katedral School's 11th grade stood lined up along the sidewalk on lower Karl Johan Street, right behind the backs of German policemen and soldiers. The idea was for the boys to execute a smart about-face just as the cortege of cars drove by. The 11th graders were going to turn their backs on Goebbels!

Ole Jacob was on messenger duty. His tiny body wriggled in and out among German uniforms as he covered a steady route between Rolf and his compatriots, between Rolf and the railway station, where red carpets had been rolled out.

The face of the station had been decorated with garlands of pine branches and a lighted "G" between German and Norwegian flags. Ole Jacob caught a glimpse of Terboven's stiff neck, as he climbed out of his car and half walked, half ran up the royal carpet. Terboven, the German high commissioner of Norway, had come to welcome Goebbels. Ole Jacob knew that the time was near, and decided to alert the others.

He was at the age which was not yet considered dangerous to those in control, neither to their safety nor their dignity. He could move about with comparative freedom, much more freely than the excessively tall Rolf, who, at seventeen, was often mistaken for nineteen or twenty. There was only a sprinkling of people on the streets. Oslo welcomed the visitor with red carpets, not with crowds.

And this was just what made the situation dangerous. The demonstrators couldn't very well disappear in the crowd when there was no crowd. The spectators who had turned up here were all enemies, every single one. As Ole Jacob ran up the sidewalk on the left side of the street, he sensed that the planned insult was not going to be easy.

"My aunt says 'hello'," he reported to Rolf. "She's arrived, so Gabrielsen is probably coming right away."

Beforehand they had agreed to call Goebbels "Gabrielsen," and Ole Jacob hoped that Rolf would understand that "Aunt" meant Terboven. Rolf didn't, but on the other hand, a couple of fellows turned around and stared intently at Terje and Rolf when they received this mysterious message.

Rolf and Terje looked at one another. What in all the world could this aunt, who had suddenly turned up, have to do with Goebbels? Ole Jacob's eyes studied the boys eagerly, searching for a sign of understanding, the conspirators' nod.

"Terboven, of course!" he whispered, giving up.

It had started to rain. The street lay gray and empty of traffic, the flag-draped station stood out against the gloom, resembling a masquerade guest in costume on a work-day morning. Suddenly the cars began to arrive. A whole cortege of vehicles swung up Karl Johan Street, accompanied by scattered shouts of "Heil!", of commands, and the odd, clapping noise of soldiers presenting arms. Goebbels sat in the first car—a small, snake-like head on his long neck. The dark eyes glittered, on the alert. It made Ole Jacob think of a rattlesnake. He saw the hint of a smile as Goebbels saluted the soldiers, and thought that a snake must have just such a queer, unpleasant smile. The next moment, the smile vanished as the row of schoolboys swung an about-face, turning their backs on him. Ole Jacob shivered, half in delight that the demonstration had succeeded, and half in fear, for in a second everything was in an uproar as the boys broke out and took to their heels in every direction. The cars were now far up the street, and where the boys had been standing, there were now shouts and confusion, as though the whole sidewalk had come to life. Everyone ran. Ole Jacob, too. Rolf's arm could be seen for a moment against the wall of a house, as he shook off two German soldiers.

Ole Jacob ran for his life. The asphalt was slippery, and he stumbled and slid, but kept on his feet and raced on. Then he discovered that he was running, not with the pursued but with the pursuers. They had caught up with him, but paid no attention to him. They were after the big boys. Several soldiers thundered by in heavy boots. Ole Jacob kept on as best he could, stupidly straight ahead. Once he had started, he was unable to stop. He thought he was saving his life. The pursued swung around the corner. The whole sidewalk joined in the chase. A fat little child, who had been standing right in the middle of the pavement, was knocked down and it appeared as if the soldiers, in the heat of the chase, would trample the youngster. Ole Jacob grabbed the screaming bundle, dragged it along a bit, lifted it up on his arm, and ran on.

The child—a girl—was crying loudly, bobbing up and down heavily. The soldiers had passed Ole Jacob now, but he staggered on, not yet aware that no one followed him. It was probably the unbearable weight of the screaming child that finally brought him to his senses. He leaned against a wall and put the little girl down. But, as she started to howl again, he once more picked her up, and spoke gently to her. Tears ran down her chubby cheeks, but she stopped crying as soon as she sat securely on his arm, and sticking two grubby fingers way inside her mouth, she regarded him with wet eyes. Far down the street ran the soldiers. In a crack between the child's hand and the wall of the house, he saw Rolf held by two soldiers. He offered no resistance.

6 *SPRING*

It turned out that only Rolf and Terje had been captured. All the rest of the boys had gotten away. But a few days later the State Police and German police trooped up at the school and fetched the other demonstrators. The principal asked if it were really the intention of the police to arrest school boys for the sake of a boyish prank, and was told that it was "a disgusting insult" that had to be punished. And police cars drove off with the entire 11th grade.

The whole city was talking about the incident, and at the Frænkel home Miriam went about with red-rimmed eyes, even though Ole Jacob told her over and over again that to be arrested was the greatest honor that could come to a boy. For him it was a terrible disappointment that no one took notice of him. What would Arnt have said if he had found out that he—Ole Jacob, half-Norwegian—had been pulled into jail for what no one else on the block had attempted: A Demonstration Against Goebbels! What would Arnt have said then!

But no one paid any attention to Ole Jacob.

One day he gathered together all his courage and went to the principal.

"I turned my back on Goebbels."

The principal looked over his eyeglasses at Ole Jacob and thought that this small back could hardly insult anyone, and patted the boy on the head.

"I don't think you should go around boasting of such things."

"I'd like so much to be arrested."

The principal smiled.

Ole Jacob, standing in front of him, didn't feel that there was anything to smile about. The others were heroes, but he, who had done the same and even more, was not. As always, when the situation was unclear to him, he pulled a handkerchief out of his pocket and blew his nose to help him breathe more easily and think more clearly. He put the handkerchief back in his pocket, gave a tentative sniff. But the situation was just as confusing as before: the principal smiled, and the soldiers had run past him.

"Is . . . is it because I'm a Jew? That no one pays any attention to me, I mean?"

The principal looked up, astonished. "What on earth makes you think that? We are living in an enlightened country, no one here makes a distinction between Jews and non-Jews. Get such thoughts out of your head."

"Very well."

As long as the principal had said that, Ole Jacob couldn't very well tell on Arnt now, even though he wished Arnt all the misery in the world.

Still he protested. "I've done just as much as all the others, stood with my back to Goebbels, only peeked a little over one shoulder. All the others were taken. Why shouldn't I . . . ?"

"Because you're eleven years old, my boy. You'll have to wait for jail," the principal said jokingly, "until you're old enough for such excitements."

The audience was over. Ole Jacob went home, disappointed.

It was the first fine day of that cold spring. The wagtail had come, trees and bushes, long held back by the cold, were now budding. Ahead of him walked a young girl in a light coat. People seemed happy.

He had no reason to be sorry for himself and he wasn't, he thought, though his heart was heavy and he still smarted from Arnt's words. He had heard similar expressions before, but never, never had they hurt so much as this time. It was as though he would never forget.

He and Emil were friends again. There wasn't an ounce of spite in Emil. Ole Jacob regretted that he had hit Emil so hard, but yesterday Ole Jacob had given his friend the old typewriter. It couldn't be used for anything, to be sure, for the roller didn't work, but Emil was happy with the gift.

Ole Jacob walked, kicking a stone ahead of him on the sidewalk. When the streetcar came, he managed to kick the stone right on the track so it was crushed. On an ordinary day, this incident would have started a whole series of experiments, which would have held his attention completely until dinnertime, in fact made him forget both time and dinner. But today nothing was any fun.

"Just look at that nose. . . ."

Funny that he couldn't forget those stupid words. He knew that his nose was long. He knew that he was a Jew, and was proud of being a Jew. But it had never occurred to him that he should be considered different from his comrades because of his race.

He knew now that if he had the same kind of turned-up, freckled nose as Emil's or Arnt's, he wouldn't have to walk down the street here feeling unhappy.

The young girl in the light coat swung around the corner. She was welcoming the summer with sheer silk stockings. Ole Jacob noticed a small, white square of paper halfway down one of her legs.

Ole Jacob realized at once what it was, and he knew that anyone else who saw it would know too. One doesn't put paper in one's stocking unless the paper is something to be hidden. She was carrying an illegal newspaper.

Ole Jacob looked around. He heard the heel plates of a German soldier on the opposite sidewalk. But it was dangerous for the girl to think she was safe, when the paper could be seen a long way off. He'd have to warn her.

"Half-Norwegian," he thought somewhat bitterly. How could anyone say that when he could feel how Norwegian he was all the way through if he but saw a good, patriotic Norwegian girl in danger.

He hated to speak to strangers, but there was no way out. He came up to her.

"Something's showing!" he whispered.

The girl, startled, didn't understand what he meant.

Funny how long it took people to catch on that way.

"You've got a hole in your heel," he tried again.

But the girl was wearing heavy shoes and socks over her stockings, so no stocking heels could be seen at all, and she began to think that the boy was crazy. But she glanced down all the same and caught sight of the folded piece of paper.

"Thanks," she said. "It's slipped down."

She busily righted a garter, fished up the square of paper.

Ole Jacob smiled at her. This little episode had cheered him and life seemed brighter now.

If luck is with me, I can still be arrested, he thought. Someone may be tortured and made to tell on me.

But, as he swung into the driveway at home, he stopped short and had to rub his eyes. On the same bench, which had overflowed the week before with bicycle wheels and parts, sat Miriam, and stooping in front of her, busy with the same bicycle, was Rolf.

* * * * *

All the boys had been released just as suddenly as they had been arrested. They told little or nothing of what had happened, and the other boys, who flocked around to hear, soon gave up questioning them. They were face-to-face here with things they did not understand, things that shouldn't be talked about. Their comrades bore no marks of injury, nonetheless they were not the same demonstrators who had lined up and turned their backs on Goebbels a few days ago.

Miriam and Rolf were together more than ever now, but seldom indoors. Most often they bicycled out of the city. Occasionally, Miriam took sketching material and paintbox with her, and taught Rolf to dabble in watercolors.

Hanne envied Rolf and Miriam. They always had fun together, always had enough to talk about, and if they were separated for a few days, as now, it only brought them closer together again.

Terje, on the other hand, Hanne couldn't figure out. If he had been difficult before, he was ten times worse now. It was as though he didn't notice or hear her at all. Still he appeared faithfully and fetched her, they still went on long bicycle trips together, or lay on the grass and watched Miriam and Rolf sketching each other. No, Hanne wasn't able to understand Terje.

One day the four of them were walking aimlessly down the street. Rolf and Miriam arm-in-arm ahead, Terje and

Hanne following, each couple by itself. The warm weather had finally come, but it was as if no one dared believe it. Most people were still perspiring in winter clothing, suspicious of such unaccustomed generosity. But the evening was warm, the air filled with the songs of invisible birds, and out from gardens and underbrush rose the smoky smell of bonfires.

"I'm probably not in love with him at all," thought Hanne, "and now that he's become a hero and everything."

She pondered over this.

"Do girls perplex him so much that he asks me out, even though he doesn't like me?" she wondered, and tried to imagine Terje walking down the street with another girl.

No, she didn't like that idea. Then she was probably in love with him all the same.

Hanne didn't feel comfortable with silences. She started talking, while Terje moped along as before, replying in single syllables.

When we go across the road, I'll just ask him why he goes walking with me, when he can't even bother to listen to what I say, thought Hanne.

They crossed the road, but she didn't ask him, neither about that nor about anything else.

The sky was too light for stars, the evening too dark for beetles and butterflies; there was little to talk about. And suddenly, just as they passed Ulleval Hospital, the question popped out of her all the same. Afterwards, she understood that it must have been to fill a pause.

"Why do you ask me to go out walking, Terje, when you never once listen to what I say? When you're so bored that it shows a long way off?"

There, now it was out. And there would be no more walks for *them*. It was like dropping a bomb, and waiting for it to explode.

"Bored? Me?" She heard Terje's astonished voice. "Me, bored? What makes you think that?"

"You're certainly not going to tell me that you're walking here, enjoying yourself?"

Terje's face looked so pained that she almost regretted her outburst. "I hear every word you say," he told her sulkily, not answering her question.

"Why, you're as silent as a fish!"

"Isn't it nice to be quiet together?" was Terje's unexpected reply.

Well, well, maybe it was nice to keep silent together, as long as Terje said so. But she couldn't understand what was so wonderful about walking here like an old married couple, just inhaling fresh air. She ought to keep quiet and see how long he would feel comfortable with this silence of his.

The steeple on Sagene Church raised its peaked, monk's cowl towards the skies. The face of the clock was unlighted because of the blackout, but still the face shone like a huge, white eye under the cowl.

"Doesn't it look like a one-eyed monk?" asked Hanne.

"What—huh? One-eyed monk?" Terje looked around. "Where do you see any one-eyed monks?"

"There. The church steeple."

"No, I don't think so. It looks like a church steeple."

As the young couple swung around the corner and approached the bridge, Hanne got ready to say goodnight, and to say that she wasn't so certain she would be free on Sundays after all. It was as though their friendship had come to a crossroad. She felt sad and a little angry too. Suddenly Terje grabbed her elbow hard, swung her around, and walked back towards the church again. He was still just as silent. Now they saw the steeple from the other side. The sky had turned completely violet.

There was something working inside of Terje, something he wanted to say and couldn't get out. He looked as if he were sorry about something. A lock of hair hung down over his forehead, but he didn't fling the stray lock back with a jerk of his head the way he usually did.

At last he spoke. "You ask if I'm enjoying myself. Did you know that it was me—me who turned in all the other boys . . . ?"

"Terje!"

"Yes, you can stare at me all right. But that's the way it is. I turned them all in, the whole class! I'm just a coward! Now you know!"

It wasn't that he had betrayed his comrades that shocked her. Anyone, even the strongest, could be moved to tell by the Gestapo, everyone knew that much. But what had happened to the cocksure, self-sufficient Terje?

"They'd been questioning Rolf and me for a long time, hour after hour, when someone came and took Rolf away.

Then they fired a shot outside the door, and right after that they brought his clothes through the room. So I thought they'd shot him because he wouldn't tell. Then they came to take me, and so I told them all the names."

Now Hanne understood. The Gestapo wasn't satisfied with frightening the boys, they had humiliated them as well.

"How disgusting."

"Yes, I am disgusting."

"No, not you. They."

"I wrote down all the names. I was out of my mind about Rolf. I was scared."

"Terje, you wouldn't have been a *friend,* if you'd remained hard after something like that. How terrible it must have been for you! How you must have suffered. And all the time I've been angry at you because I thought you were too conceited to talk to me."

"I haven't anything to be conceited about. Our idea was stupid from the very beginning. It's no achievement to turn your back on a man."

"I think it was wonderful of all of you. Courageous. The only right thing to do."

"The next time we'll certainly plan better," said Terje bitterly. "From now on we'll be much more dangerous."

"And you say you're a coward! Oh Terje, you're wonderful!"

"You mean you really don't think it was so wrong then? Oh, you ought to know what a hell I've been through!"

"As if the Gestapo couldn't force a name out of a schoolboy. Why you *are* a schoolboy, Terje."

"Yes, I am a schoolboy. But I'm a fool, too."

"You are not! You ought to know what I'm like. Ugh! I even make *myself* sick at times. Me, wanting to be popular —with you, with everyone. Yes, even with that stuck-up Monica, whom I can't stand. You should know what I'm really like."

A wonderful confidence had sprung up between them. Suddenly they could talk for hours.

Terje poured out all that was bothering him, all that had troubled him like a nightmare for over a week. There are two ways to show a girl you love her: Either you can sit up on your high horse and do tricks for her, impress her with your prowess. Or else you can reveal your true self. Terje had tried both ways. Now they were talking at the same time, one confession giving way to the other.

It was almost completely dark when Hanne came home. She intended to sneak up the stairs to the attic, then saw that her parents were still up. They were raking and burning leaves in the little, squeezed-in garden.

"Well, I never! Why are you out so late?"

"We should be saying that to you," said her father. "But you know, it's nice burning leaves in the dark."

Hanne hung on the fence and watched her parents. They suddenly looked so sweet, as if they were playing doll's house.

"I picked some flowers for you," said Hanne, and held out a warm, crushed, withered bunch. "Found them on a dump."

"Thanks. Won't the lady come inside? We haven't seen you in a long time."

Hanne banged the garden gate behind her, went up the path with long strides, as though she were wading through tall grass.

"Why Hanne! How little you have on!" scolded her mother. "You know that spring is dangerous. Aren't you chilly?"

"Do I look like I'm freezing? Now, if you'd asked if I were hungry . . ."

"I'll pour you a cup of hot tea. Come."

They went indoors to where the supper table was still set. "Fresh bread!" Hanne said enthusiastically.

"My, how cheerful you are tonight," her mother said as she came in with the steaming kettle, and looked a little searchingly at her daughter.

"Cheerful!" Hanne scoffed at that inadequate word. "I'm more than cheerful. I'm in love!"

And when both her parents turned bewildered faces towards her, she swung the bread-knife triumphantly over her head.

"It happened this evening!"

7 AGDA GETS MARRIED

Summer—and with it came separations. Mr. Hoygard bicycled on Orland, and found out, with a heavy heart, that the Germans were dumping the rich topsoil into the sea to reclaim the land, and building airports where he had played as a child.

Terje and Rolf embarked on a hiking tour of the Hardanger Mountains, and made plans for the illegal activities of the autumn and winter.

The Frænkels were in town. Dr. Frænkel, who kept in constant touch with London, was tied to Oslo. And the rest of the family had their hands full with preparations for Agda's wedding, and fitting up her new home. Georg's frightening predictions about persecution of the Jews after Goebbels' visit had not come true.

The one who enjoyed herself least that summer was Hanne. Alone, she bicycled along the wind-swept roads on Orland, where all her favorite old haunts had been closed off by rusty barbed wire. Terje didn't write from the mountains, and the few letters she did receive during the summer were just as uncommunicative as he himself had been before the Spring. The new fine intimacy did not find its way into the letters. Hanne felt forgotten and far away. Finally, early in August, she received a letter from Miriam:

Dear Hanne,

Now it has happened. Agda is married, and how I wish, wish that you could have seen her as a bride. Georg wanted us to observe all the old customs, and I think you would have agreed that a synagogue wedding is lovely.

My shoes were much too tight, for I had outgrown them long ago, so I kicked them off, while we sat waiting for the bride, because I couldn't bear having them on. Papa was deeply moved, and when he is moved, he becomes more absent-minded than ever. When the time came to walk down the aisle, he took very long strides. So poor Agda had to run beside him. And Georg, who only had eyes for Agda, became so enraptured with his lovely bride, who practically ran up to him, that he hardly knew what he was doing. He probably thought she was running to

*him out of longing, but Agda was really angry just then;
I could see her anger clearly, because I know her so well,
and she isn't half so romantic as Georg. She was annoyed
because Papa was so thoughtless, and so long-legged, and
didn't remember that a bride should walk slowly.*

*But when the wedding was over, and Agda and Georg
were really married, I became so moved, too, that I forgot
my shoes, and walked all the way out to the car in my
stocking feet. You see, my feet were not quite touching
the ground, for I had never seen anything like Georg's face.
And it was Ole Jacob who discovered that I was sitting in
my stockings. And I couldn't go back without shoes myself,
so Papa asked Ole Jacob to do it, and he scowled furiously
at people who laughed at him when he came out of the
synagogue with a pair of white satin shoes in his hands.*

*The wedding dinner was held at the home of Georg's
parents, as we didn't have enough room. And there was
quite a disturbance at the table, for we had invited the
twins on the first floor along with their parents, who have
been so kind to us. And while Georg's father was making
a speech, the twins crawled under the table and pinched
our legs. And their mother said that if we just ignored
them, and pretended that nothing was going on, they would
soon grow tired of doing it. So we sat there and waited
for the twins to grow tired of pinching our legs. Georg
was quite furious, and many others were too. But we didn't
say anything, of course, for the twins' parents have been
extremely wonderful to us.*

And now Georg and Agda are really married, and live

in their lovely apartment. But if I read this letter over again, I'll never send it, for it tells more about the twins and tight shoes than about the wedding.

Aren't you coming home soon?

Your,
Miriam

8 ROLF'S MOTHER

The first Saturday after everyone was back in town, Rolf invited Miriam, Hanne and Terje with him out to Enebakk, where his parents had bought a farm. Rolf's mother had worked constantly during the spring and summer, and now the gray, bare cottage had become a red-painted dream house with rustic furniture and roses growing up the wall.

Miriam had never met a lady as elegant as Rolf's mother. At a time when all clothing was beginning to look made-over and improved on, and each improvement only succeeded in giving the garment more of a make-shift appearance, Mrs.

Kjeldsen looked as though she had stepped right out of the glossy pages of *Vogue* or *Harper's Bazaar,* so simple and tasteful was her dress. Each time Miriam was in Rolf's home, she thought: My, today Mrs. Kjeldsen is even prettier than usual. How does she do it? And Mrs. Kjeldsen, who found Miriam's teen-age admiration a pleasant excitement, accepted it as a matter of course; yes, she even encouraged it. She had a way of flirting with everyone, and often stood on tiptoe and ruffled Rolf's hair to show how tiny she was beside her unreasonably tall son, as if she were the mother of an out-and-out joke. And Miriam was aglow with admiration. She copied Rolf's mother in secret, sketched her and hung the drawing on the curtain alongside Cary Grant, never put on a blouse or arranged the flowers in the room without wondering whether Mrs. Kjeldsen would like it that way.

For Mrs. Kjeldsen was surrounded by beauty. The apartment in town was more a flattering frame for her than a home. It would have been a crime to take a nap on her fine sofa. The carpets were so pale that one was afraid to walk on them. Everybody preferred going around them, so that the Kjeldsen family usually moved in angles and squares across the floor. It was difficult for Rolf and his father to have everything so elegant, but for Miriam, who loved beauty, Rolf's home was the nicest place she knew. She enjoyed sitting still amidst the harmonious colors, enjoyed following Mrs. Kjeldsen with her eyes when she went over and turned on a lamp in the corner—not because light was needed, but because the glow from the lampshade made the room lovelier.

The only thing that fell outside the pattern in this home was Rolf himself. Mrs. Kjeldsen wasn't able to work on him. Rolf's father was a color symphony in blue and gray, or brown and beige. Mrs. Kjeldsen herself picked out his ties, shirts, jackets and trousers. But no one could call Rolf a symphony in color. He was just a collection of spots and tears, and he wasn't at home in his clothes until they were old and worn. Comfortable, he called them then. And Mrs. Kjeldsen had the job of lengthening and letting out, so that favorite pants and jackets could keep pace with his constantly growing arms and legs.

Miriam could see that Rolf did not at all conform to his mother's unblemished surroundings. But Mrs. Kjeldsen had long since given him up, regarding his size and attire as a joke at which she laughed and shook her head. But she made no further attempt to dress him up.

She ruled her husband with a firm hand. When the war came, she insisted that he buy the farm, even though the only thing he was interested in was sailing. Then, when the Germans took his sailboat and even the car, she praised him for having been far-sighted when he purchased the farm. And every Saturday the family took the bus to Enebakk, along with a crowd of Rolf's friends. In the winter they went skiing, in the summer they helped with the haying, walked or went swimming in a muddy forest pond, where water lilies and white birches grew. And in the meantime, Mrs. Kjeldsen, wearing sunglasses and gardening gloves, beautified the farm until it was completely changed.

It was the first Saturday after Rolf had come home from

the mountains that he invited Miriam, Hanne and Terje along with him to Enebakk. It was mid-August, and very warm. Mrs. Kjeldsen herself took the girls up to the light guest room, where the summer skies could be seen through a veil of white lace curtains. In the evening everybody sat out of doors under a linden tree and ate crawfish, and Mr. Kjeldsen máde a speech in honor of Rolf, for it was his birthday. In the tree hung golden paper lanterns, and they lighted up the dark August night like giant fireflies so that Miriam couldn't stop looking at them. Behind the house lay a bit of meadow which Mrs. Kjeldsen would not allow them to mow because it was full of daisies. Here the two young couples walked afterwards, and it was all so romantic that Hanne and Miriam became noble, and forgave Terje and Rolf for the letters they hadn't written during their vacation.

The next day Terje and Rolf helped the manager of the farm put up a fence, and Hanne and Miriam explored the woods with the farm dog. It was an old, fat hound which answered to the name of "Hopla," even though she could neither hop nor run. But from her earliest days, she loved trips in the woods, and in her excitement almost knocked Miriam and Hanne down, as if the dog thought they were going rabbit hunting.

It was a hot day, full of the smell of timber and sun-warmed pine. A well-beaten, brown path led through the blueberry patches. Mrs. Kjeldsen had fixed a lunch for the girls, and in a few hours they had taken a swim, sun bathed, eaten blueberries, and almost killed a viper that had escaped at the last moment. And Miriam had picked flowers and arranged them in an artistic bouquet, which she wrapped in moss and watered in the stream from time to time.

Hanne laughed at her. "What are you going to do with them?"

"Give them to Mrs. Kjeldsen, of course. They're exactly her colors."

"Why, she has flowers in every vase already."

"Doesn't matter. These are going to stand on the folding table in the parlor, against the pale blue wallpaper."

Hanne groaned. "You're trying to outdo Mrs. Kjeldsen."

"A house certainly can't be *too* pretty!" Miriam retorted irritably. Mrs. Kjeldsen was the only subject she and Hanne disagreed about.

"Mrs. Kjeldsen is the cleverest person I know," continued Miriam. "Can you imagine anything so lovely as that party for Rolf last night! Just thinking up a party like that . . ."

"Of course. Lovely! Lovely! My stars! But she doesn't think about anything else. The objects in her home are more important than her family. I mean, when a pillow mustn't be squeezed and a rug mustn't be walked on. . . . She's got prettiness on the brain. Next she'll probably paint the fence pink and tie ribbons on the hens!"

Miriam didn't condescend to answer. Hanne simply didn't understand. She had no respect for pretty pillows. The love of flowers and beauty were something that Rolf's mother and Miriam had in common.

But Hanne didn't stop. "One shouldn't lie on one's stomach for one's mother-in-law, either."

"Mother-in-law! Listen to you!"

"You needn't pretend! Terje and I are going to get engaged one day and so are the two of you. If Mrs. Kjeldsen gives her permission."

Now Miriam laughed. "And why shouldn't Mrs. Kjeldsen give us her permission? She likes me. She's said so herself."

"Of course she likes you. But I don't know. Mrs. Kjeldsen has her own plans for everyone and everything. Rolf, and the farm, and the sofa in the parlor."

They spoke no more then about Mrs. Kjeldsen. Hopla started giving them trouble. After hobbling ahead on the path towards imaginary rabbits, and over-estimating her own strength for two hours, she now hung far behind, lay down flat, or crawled along with her tongue hanging out. And when the girls and dog reached the shadeless, sun-baked road, Hopla's panting sounded like a motor.

The girls decided to take a shortcut through the fenced-in pasture, which lay up to the farm. They put the leash on Hopla and found a place in the fence through which they could squeeze Hopla's fat body. As soon as they came into the shade of the trees, Hopla apparently felt better. And then, after taking a bath in a slimy, stagnant brook, which had a bad smell, the dog became so refreshed that she shook herself, flicking water over the girls' summer dresses, and then, wet and long-bellied, she lumbered ahead on the path. Miriam and Hanne breathed easier.

But they had forgotten about the cows. When the girls emerged from a glade in the pasture, where six cows and a young bull were grazing, Hopla started barking and worrying the animals, and before the girls knew what was happening, the whole herd had started after them. Miriam got out the leash again and fastened it to the collar of the excited dog—and how a rabbit hound can bark when it gets started!—and together they hopped over fallen trees and branches with Hopla baying on the leash.

At the far end of the pasture there was an enclosure where the cows usually came, late in the afternoon, to be milked. All the paths in the woods led to this enclosure, and suddenly the girls were inside with the herd practically at their heels, while Hopla was barking so that it was impossible to hear anything else.

"Over the fence, quick!" shouted Hanne. "Hopla will have to take care of herself. Hurry!"

The girls climbed up the low, netting fence, which creaked under their feet, and tumbled, shouting and laughing, down on the other side. They were saved.

But Hopla wasn't. Squeezed up in a corner, she stood barking furiously at the cows, as they came closer and closer.

"Hopla! Shut up, you idiot!" shouted Miriam. But she wasn't heard. "Oh Hanne, we can't leave her there."

They bent over the low fence, and grabbed Hopla around the stomach. She started kicking as soon as she was lifted, but her fur was wet and slippery after the bath, and the girls couldn't hold on. The cows were now inside the enclosure, and had slowed down, but the young bull took a few steps closer and bellowed angrily.

"He'll kill her!" shrieked Hanne. "Hopla's too heavy for us!"

Their fright gave them strength. They grabbed Hopla again and pulled. The warm, heavy body was lifted up. Hopla neither barked nor kicked, but a growl rumbled in her throat as she was being lifted towards the edge of the fence.

"Ow! She's sliding out of my hands! She's too heavy!" groaned Hanne. Her hands slipped from the wet fur.

Hopla yelped and wriggled under the hands of her rescuers, and was about to slide back to the mud and cow horns on the other side of the fence.

Suddenly the herd moved even closer to watch what was happening, no doubt.

Hanne squeaked with fright. "She'll be killed! They'll trample her down . . ."

Once more, the girls grabbed Hopla. With a tremendous yank, they hauled the wriggling body over so forcefully the fence creaked. All three tumbled on top of each other, the girls underneath, exhausted by their efforts and their laughter.

Their clothes were muddy from the brook where Hopla had bathed, sandals and legs were smeared with dirt from the enclosure. Hanne and Miriam looked at each other, but couldn't say a word for laughing.

A cow sniffed at Miriam's flowers—which she had dropped in her fright—blew hot breath on them, and licked them with a blue tongue.

"Stop!" cried Miriam. "Those flowers are not for you, you

idiot! You've got the whole woods full!" She was halfway over the fence again.

"Hey, wait," Hanne shouted. "You're not going in there with them again! Have you lost your mind?" She caught Miriam's dress.

"Let me go! I've got to get those flowers for Mrs. Kjeldsen." She was already down on the other side, wading to the flowers which lay in the middle of a puddle.

She was wearing a red dress, and she scolded at the young bull which bucked and turned its bloodshot eyes on her. The flies were bothering it. Miriam was scared and wondered it she'd ever get out of that muddy corner full of warm cow bodies. The bull moved again, and she let out a yell, threw the flowers over the fence, and flinging herself against it, climbed for her life in the shaky squares.

In her excitement, Hanne grabbed at Miriam, at her hair and her dress, wherever Hanne could get a hold. Neither girl realized that the cows had completely lost interest in them now that Hopla was out of reach. They stood, mooing wearily in the afternoon sun, pressing themselves heavy with milk against the fence, waiting for someone to come and milk them.

"That's the most idiotic thing I ever saw!" gasped Hanne. "You could have picked fresh flowers."

"Not as pretty." Miriam rearranged the bouquet. "Here are oxeye daisies, and marigolds, and the big bluebells Mrs. Kjeldsen likes so much. She said so yesterday."

"Oh, there's Terje!" Hanne started to run, plunged through

raspberry bushes and nettles, and small thickets in the direction of a boy who was waving a pair of bathing trunks from a distance. "Miriam, we'll certainly have time for a swim before dinner. Hurry!" she shouted back.

"I just want to put the flowers in water first!" Miriam called after her. But Hanne didn't hear. Forgotten were Miriam and the cows, and the fright and Mrs. Kjeldsen's flowers. Hanne ran over new-mown fields with Hopla trying to keep up with her and both vanished behind a rack of hay drying in the sun.

Miriam laughed and looked at the flowers, which showed signs of withering. As long as she had risked her neck for them, she'd better see about getting them in water. She started running, flew on light sandals up towards the house, through the apple orchard to the veranda. The laughter was still in her throat, bubbling up whenever she thought of Hanne's perspiring, dirty face when the girls had been struggling with Hopla.

Slightly out of breath she reached the flagstones in front of the steps, put the bouquet down on the bottom step, and hastily arranged her hair before showing herself to Mrs. Kjeldsen's beauty-loving eyes. How did she look, as a matter of fact? She stroked her hair and cheek. Both were muddy.

In the still of the afternoon, the buzz of voices from the living-room resounded in the garden. She paid no attention to the conversation but heard the tinkle of ice cubes and knew punch was being poured into tall glasses. It sounded cool and refreshing.

"I can't take you seriously when you talk like that,

Mother," came Rolf's voice, and Miriam, combing her hair quickly, wondered what it was that Rolf couldn't take seriously.

"Besides, Rolf, you know it is risky to be too friendly with Jews these days," Mrs. Kjeldsen said in her usual calm voice. "You could get us all into trouble. . . ."

"Oh Mother, no! Don't say that at least. . . ." Rolf's voice was raised, and sounded clearly in the garden. "You want me to break with Miriam because of Hitler! Because of those mad ideas of his. . . . You want me to be a coward, a. . . ."

Rolf's father, evidently feeling that his son was on the point of going too far now, broke in. Mr. Kjeldsen had a half teasing, half protecting way of dealing with his family.

"Rolf, you know your mother always sees a potential daughter-in-law in every girl you meet. She always has— ever since you were three years old. So what she really means . . ."

"Nonsense, Conrad! You know perfectly well what I mean. I only want to vaccinate Rolf a little, so he won't fall in love too hard. He is still young for love. Well, Miriam *is* sweet. Very sweet. But Rolf feels like her protector, and that is fatal. He should not make a choice for a lifetime yet. Can't you see that? She is sweet now, but think when she gets older! Think when she becomes a fat old Jew-lady . . ."

Miriam's knees grew weak. She sank down on the step beside the flowers. She wanted to get up and run, but couldn't. She would not have believed that words could stab so!

"Fat . . . old . . . Jew-lady." So that's what Mrs. Kjeldsen thought of her while she was being sweet and nice and hospitable.

"Yes, they become that way when they grow old . . ." ' said Mrs. Kjeldsen's cultivated voice.

Miriam sat as if in a daze, heard a chair being kicked angrily over the floor, heard Rolf answer, but not what he said. Short, angry words. Suddenly she realized that he was coming out on the veranda, that he would understand that she had heard every word, that it was too late to get away.

Rolf stopped short when he caught sight of her. His face flushed. He stood still, opened his mouth, found nothing to say, closed it again.

Miriam sat on the bottom step, her face and dress dirty. She resembled most a bird that had fallen out of its nest and been hurt.

Someone in the living room rose and shoved a chair away from the table. Miriam jumped up in panic, plunged down through the kitchen garden and into the woods as if demons were at her heels.

But now Rolf came to life and was after her in great strides, catching up with her by the fence. He took her by the arm.

"Miriam . . ."

"Let me go!" She wrenched away, and headed down the path. Rolf let her go but followed. She didn't run fast for she was crying.

Not until they were well in the woods did he catch up with her, take her by both wrists and hold her fast.

"Miriam . . . listen to me! You're not going to take that nonsense seriously?"

She twisted to free herself. Then he put his arm around her waist, held her close to him, and kissed her wherever he could touch her wet, dirty face.

"Miriam, you can't just keep on walking in the woods. Where are you going?"

"Oh, I don't know where I want to go . . ."

He kissed her again. She calmed down a little.

"Come, let's sit and talk together," he said.

They sat down on a wind-felled fir tree. He pulled out a handkerchief and wiped away tears and dirt, and then showed her the handkerchief. She laughed a little, to his great relief. He put his arm around her shoulders, felt how tiny they were and remembered his mother's words.

He was ashamed for his mother.

Fat Jew-lady! The phrase sounded so vulgar, he thought. Words like that branded themselves inside, and never were forgotten. He wanted to comfort Miriam but didn't know how. He eased her head against his shoulder and sat so that he was supporting her comfortably.

"You're not to feel sorry for me!" she said suddenly, angrily.

"No, are you crazy? As a matter of fact I think you're a little stupid. Actually, I am angry with you for trying to run away from me."

Again she laughed briefly and again he pressed her head against his shoulder.

As if this lively, vital girl would ever be big and fat! Idiotic to say such a thing.

She had quieted now and sat with her eyes closed. Occasionally she sighed. He was sitting twisted in an awkward position, pressed down on one side, but he did not mind if *she* was comfortable. It was so quiet that he could hear all the little sounds from the woods. A squirrel danced across the glade, close by, but Miriam didn't stir. He wondered if she were asleep. He had been in love many times, but not like this. It was as though all of him had turned into a shoulder which supported her, a crooked and tired shoulder, but still it was wonderful.

At last she looked up. "Can . . . could I get you all into trouble?"

"Nonsense, Miriam. The Nazis are hopeless with Jews. We all know that. But so far they haven't been much interested in what stupid Norwegians say about Jews."

This seemed to calm her for a while. Then another wound started bleeding.

"She wanted . . . to vaccinate you against me—as if I were a disease."

"She will never manage that," said Rolf bluntly.

She leaned her head against his shoulder again. "If only it hadn't been her . . . if only it hadn't been your mother, I mean, who said it. I've always admired her so . . ."

He stroked her arm gently.

"You know, Miriam, even if my mother doesn't like . . . even if she does have one thing or another against the Jews, why she still likes you." He spoke loudly, delighted at finally having found something to say that would comfort her, something which was completely true.

But then the tears started sliding down her wet cheeks again.

"I'd almost rather she liked Jews and not me," she sobbed.

A little later, when she noticed how disappointed he was, she put her arms around his neck.

"Mother isn't the way you think she is after what happened today. Underneath she's very kind, I'll have you know. When she wants to . . . vaccinate me against you, as she says, it's not so much because you're a Jewess as it is because I'm young. She doesn't like 'childhood engagements,' as she calls them. But it would never occur to her not to let you visit us, or any such nonsense."

No, thought Miriam bitterly, for Norwegians did not keep Jews out of their home and Mrs. Kjeldsen didn't want to be out of fashion, whether the fashion was clothes or opinions. Miriam closed her eyes and bit her lip to keep from crying again. Mrs. Kjeldsen had fallen from a pedestal, a high and fine pedestal where she had been beauty queen and mother in place of Miriam's own. She had tumbled too far ever to rise so high again. Maybe she was kind, or, at any rate, amiable. But she was not anyone to worship.

"No, she probably won't stop me from visiting you. But she'll put up with me, just the way she puts up with the spots on your clothes."

"Miriam . . . you mustn't say things like that."

"It's true, Rolf. And she's not alone in thinking as she does, I'll have you know."

"You know very well, Miriam, that for me it doesn't make an ounce of difference whether a girl is a Jewess or not, so long as she's sweet, and fine, and a good companion . . . and . . ." He searched for a word, ". . . wonderful, the way you are."

Miriam smiled.

He had been afraid she would want to run back to town on the very first bus so as not to see his mother again. But he was pleasantly surprised. She tossed her head when he asked if she would rather go home.

"I'm not a child, just because I blubber," she said. "Do you think I want to make a scene, and run home like a spoiled baby? Don't worry, Rolf. I'll be all right."

And she was.

At dinner she wore her prettiest dress. And there was no trace of tears. She talked and laughed with the others. The evening was pleasantly cool. Again the lanterns were lit in the branches. And only Rolf noticed that Miriam laughed louder than usual.

Mrs. Kjeldsen had swept the withered flowers on the veranda step into the dustpan. And Hanne did not notice that Miriam's bouquet was not in the house. But then, there were so many flowers in Mrs. Kjeldsen's house.

9 *TAKEN BY SURPRISE*

Hanne had long since given Miriam back the key to "The Old Court," and after the summer vacation, they had fallen into the habit of doing their homework together. The attic room was an undisturbed place, and now that Agda had married, there was no one to ask Miriam what she did in the evenings.

And up to now it had always gone well.

One day, at the end of October, they were sitting as usual up in the attic room. They were quite alone in the house. Hanne's father was at the factory and her mother at her sewing club. The girls had almost finished their lessons. Miriam was getting ready to go home and fix supper.

They had been sitting with blankets wrapped around their knees. It was icy cold in the attic, and there was nothing to make a fire with. Miriam yawned. She was shivering because she was tired as well as cold. There was no Agda to fix breakfast and straighten up in the two small rooms any more and most of the work fell on Miriam. And last night there had been considerable disturbance and little sleep. The neighboring house had been raided. In the middle of the night the Frænkels had been awakened by the terrifying sound of cars stopping outside in the dark. The Gestapo had come to arrest Arnt's mother, Mrs. Andresen. But they had been cheated, for by the time they had reached the second floor of the big, white villa, both Mrs. Andresen and the boy had managed to climb down by way of the veranda. All that night they lay hidden behind a wood-pile in the garden, and in the morning they got clothing from the neighbors.

"Ole Jacob is in such low spirits today," said Miriam. "Not that he and Arnt are such good friends any more, but Ole Jacob probably thinks Arnt should have gotten clothing from him, his closest neighbor, instead of going to a boy farther away. Arnt is used to climbing up to our balcony. He likes that kind of sport. But this time he didn't. Ole Jacob feels left out."

Hanne rubbed her hands to warm them. "Strange they came to take such a lonely widow. How can she be dangerous to anybody?"

"Oh, I'm not the least surprised. Mrs. Andresen has been in the underground for quite a while, but unlike others she *talked* about it. That really is asking for trouble. Besides now the Gestapo are arresting anyone. The next will probably be Miss Lepsoe."

Hanne couldn't help laughing. "Then she'll probably tell them how short-necked and pot-bellied they are. Have you gotten your dress?"

"No, she's never put me off before the way she has this time. She's been busy with two brides, she says. I'll probably have to be a bride myself to get my dress."

"Probably." Pause. "Mrs. Kjeldsen says she sees so little of you nowadays."

"Oh, she certainly doesn't miss me."

"Why isn't Mrs. Kjeldsen so wonderful any more?" Hanne wanted to know. But Miriam couldn't bring herself to tell Hanne about that day when her pretty flowers had ended in the trash can. Not even now, so long afterwards. She was going to say something trivial about having less time now that she was taking art lessons, but suddenly she sat still and listened.

"What's the matter?" asked Hanne.

"Shhhh! Was that a car that stopped outside . . . ?"

The girls kept silent for a moment. Suddenly a car door slammed. They both got up.

"It's probably only a truck from the factory," said Hanne.

"What would a truck be doing here at 'The Old Court'? I hate cars that stop. Cars should keep moving."

"Or else the director is coming to talk with Papa." Hanne was prone to wishful thinking.

"The director no longer has a car—neither he nor anybody else. You know that very well," said Miriam irritably. All the unpleasantness of the night before had returned with the slam of a car door.

From the front hall suddenly came the sound of someone kicking at the door.

"It's the twins!" said Hanne, trying to joke. "Now they've found your hideout!"

Miriam brushed the hair from her forehead, her hand trembling a hit. "Hanne, please go and see," she begged.

Hanne went out on the landing, but remained there indecisively. "Miriam, come out here. What do you make of this?"

The doorknob was being rattled, the bell was ringing, someone was kicking the panel of the door. The girls hung over the railing, and stared down the half-darkened hallway. It was like a funnel which amplified the noise.

They stared at each other. "What'll we do, Miriam?"

It is almost impossible to ignore a bell that continues ringing. Finally, Hanne did what one usually does when a doorbell rings; she opened the door.

"State Police! Why didn't you open the door?"

"We . . . I . . . was up in the attic."

"Does Dr. Frænkel live here?"

From the top of the stairs Miriam heard the name and it struck her like the blow of a whip. What kind of a mess had she gotten herself into now? Good heavens, what had she done? Come straight back here where she shouldn't be? What had she done?

"Dr. Frænkel moved a year ago," came Hanne's clear voice. She no longer stammered. She stood right on the threshold as if, with her presence, she could keep the enemy out.

"Where did he go?"

"I don't know."

"Don't know! Don't know!" mimicked a voice. A hand shoved Hanne to one side, and two young men in State Police uniforms, and a German dressed in civilian clothes tramped into the front hall. They caught sight of Miriam at once.

"Who's that?"

There was a pause. Miriam shut her mouth around that dangerous name of hers.

"That's my friend," said Hanne. "You frightened her with all that noise you made."

"What's her name?"

This time there was no hesitancy. "Inger Rasmussen." Hanne almost shouted the name. Neither then nor later did she knew where it came from.

Miriam stood, pale and dark-eyed, on the stairs. She resembled a slim, gypsy girl. Never before had Hanne seen her friend look so un-Norwegian.

"Identity card!"

That was an order not to be ignored.

"I'll . . . get it."

Miriam turned and ran stumbling up the stairs.

Inside the room she found her bag, tore up the identity card and stuffed it into the cold stove. With a match she set fire to the scraps.

When she returned, the police had gone into the living room. They turned on lights without lowering the blackout curtains, wrote the names of the present tenants, pulled out drawers. They seemed to have forgotten Miriam. They were three quite ordinary young men to look at, churlish, overly sure of themselves.

"Inger!" called Hanne from a window. Miriam didn't move. "Inger!" Hanne beckoned to her. "Come and help me with the string to this blackout curtain. Say you left your identity card in your desk at school," she whispered. "If they remember to ask you about it, I mean."

The German, who spoke Norwegian, asked Hanne to call her parents, but when she said they had gone to the movies, he joined the others in the smoking-room, and started rummaging in the desk drawers there.

So far everything had gone better than could be expected. Then something terrible happened.

Through the open front door, a woman walked in with a package in her hand. She went into the front hall, carelessly knocking at the open door to attract attention, put the package down on the dresser between clothes brushes and mirrors, and announced in a loud, shrill voice:

"Here's the dress for Miss Frænkel!"

The woman was Miss Lepsoe!

To Miriam it seemed as though her name exploded like a hand grenade. Automatically she closed her eyes. Stupidly and willfully she had led her family and the Hoygards into disaster. What good was it now that the Frænkels had squeezed themselves into two small uncomfortable rooms for over a year! She dared not imagine what would happen now. Everything was lost, and it was her fault. When she opened her eyes again, she saw Miss Lepsoe standing on the threshold, nodding to her and Hanne. She had on a large, black hat, and was blinking, blinded by the light.

"Why, I just had to look in on you," she said. "I thought you were all out of your minds when I saw how you'd turned on the lights without drawing down the blackout curtains. Lucky there was no policeman nearby or you'd have a nice big fine to pay. Are you alone?"

"Yes," said Miriam.

"I might have known. Well, I just thought I'd drop the dress by. Had a bad conscience because I took so long. There's a bill in the package. You can come by with the money when it's convenient. Well, goodbye now."

Her high heels clicked into the front hall. Almost at the door she turned, jokingly pointed an accusing finger. "The two of you look as though you had guilty consciences." Then she left without closing the door.

Miriam had expected someone to grab her and drag her away. But nothing happened. The enemy was in the smoking-room, rummaging around in Papa's half-empty drawers. They had not heard Miss Lepsoe! Right after she left, the three men came out into the front hall, and noticing the package, tore it open. The bill, with her name on it, fell to the floor. She hadn't once thought of the telltale bill. She wasn't good for anything. It was as though all her thoughts and movements were paralyzed.

Suddenly one of the police turned to her.

"Identity card, girl! Where is it?"

Miriam leaned against the wall for support. He loomed over her, tall and broad shouldered.

"I must have left it in my desk at school," she said. Good that Hanne had prompted her. "In . . . in one of the books," Miriam added on her own.

"You're to carry it with you; you know that all right! What did you say your name was?

Miriam couldn't for the life of her remember what her name was—"Inger Andreassen," she stammered. She had completely forgotten what Hanne had said. But fortunately, he had too.

"You've got such a long nose. You're not a Jew, are you?"

He came closer, stared suspiciously at her face. Miriam pressed both hands against the wall. She was dizzy. The man started swaying back and forth before her eyes. The white bill, with her name on it, lay face up on the floor.

"What do you know about Jews?" said the other State Policeman. He had a broad, sun-tanned face, and strong fists, and resembled a farm boy who had just arrived in the city.

"What do I know about Jews? Me, who can smell one all the way across the street!" The voice was just as crude as the words.

But it appeared that the "farm boy" was the leader.

"O.K. Now we've finished here!" he shouted. "Let's go."

The others moved towards the front door. The "farm boy" bent down, picked up the bill, and read the name. Unobtrusively he slipped it into Miriam's hand.

"Burn it," he said softly.

The door slammed behind him.

Hanne and Miriam stared at each other for a moment, breathing deeply. Then Miriam collapsed against the wall and sank to the floor. But Hanne hauled her up.

"You must go home!" she said emphatically. "You must go home right away!" She leaped up the stairs after Miriam's coat and dressed her friend as if she were a child. "You must hurry as fast as you can! See here, take that wretched dress with you!" Hanne threw it, unwrapped, over Miriam's arm. "What a disastrous dress! But all went well! Run now. The police have gone . . . all of them. Oh Miriam . . ." Hanne threw her arms around her friend, and hugged her. "I'll call Rolf," she said comfortingly.

"Yes, call Rolf!"

Hanne pushed Miriam gently out of the door and stood looking after her.

As Miriam ran through the streets, she kept slipping and stumbling. She hugged the dress tightly against her, and ran until she was breathless. It was completely dark now and fortunately she met no one. Once she stopped to catch her breath when, from the other sidewalk, a voice shouted to her. She didn't hear what the voice said, but it reminded her of another one she had just heard.

"I can smell a Jew all the way across the street . . ."

She started running again, stumbling and breathing hard.

Her bag, with money in it, lay behind in Hanne's attic room. Neither of the girls had thought of money for the street car. She cried a little when it occurred to her, then she stumbled on through the darkness.

It was quiet in the house when she finally got there. In the neighboring villa, where Arnt and his mother had lived, a light shone from an uncurtained window. A lamp had been forgotten.

She dived into the living room.

"Oh Papa, I'm sorry, I've been so stupid . . ." She stopped, out of breath. "They've been home to arrest us."

Her father stood bent over a knapsack.

"I know," he said calmly. "Rolf has called. We can't stay here any longer. We must go."

10 *THE FLIGHT*

Terje drove them. Terje borrowed his father's delivery truck, hid the three of them in the roomy back compartment, as if they were merchandise, lashed the doors so that air could come in through a crack. And drove with a forged zone pass, a forged driving permit, and a newly acquired driver's license in his pocket.

They were heading for Sweden, the land of freedom. Rolf sat beside Terje on the front seat. Outside the ground was covered with frost and the temperature was dropping. Tiny grains of drifting snow beat against the windshield. The wiper scraped monotonously, and the headlights shone on a white road with black tracks. The young men talked to keep themselves awake. Rolf was the map-reader.

Inside the compartment, with her back to him, sat Miriam, hidden away like forbidden cargo. Occasionally when the car stopped for the boys to get their bearings or read a sign-post in the dark, it seemed to Rolf that he could feel Miriam's fright. He longed to comfort her, to hold her close beside him, but, no, she had to be stowed away like a criminal. And the only crime of this lovely girl was that she'd been born a Jewess.

The plan was to drive the long way to a certain place near the Swedish border where experienced guides daily—or at least nightly—risked their lives to take refugees out of Norway. German soldiers regularly policed the border, and there were numerous sentry posts, but the forest was so dense, and the guides so clever, that more often than not they managed to evade their pursuers.

The roads were not so regularly patrolled as the border, so they hoped to be lucky. They had made up a long story about a funeral, and had the forged zone pass ready in case the truck should be stopped.

They drove through Lillestrom, peering about on all sides to make certain no uniforms should suddenly appear and ask if they had permission to drive in the district. But the streets were deserted, not a light shining and the people lay asleep behind blacked-out windows. The few soldiers they passed showed no interest in the truck.

Rolf had to get out and peer at signposts almost every time they came to a fork in the road.

One hundred kilometers. One hundred kilometers if they drove straight to the clearing in Setskog without making any wrong turns. The distance was no problem at all, Terje thought. There and back again in one night, so the delivery truck could drive its regular routes again in the morning without any suspicion of illegal transport. But Terje hadn't had much experience behind a steering wheel. He had only received his driver's license the week before. And Rolf didn't own a license at all; Norwegians were not permitted to drive cars and use up fuel except in very special circumstances.

It was annoying how often they had to stop to see if they were on the right road. There was no one to ask in the middle of the night—no one to help them if anything went wrong. Terje had to get out every now and then to stoke the generator. There was, of course, no other fuel than these miserable wooden cubes, so ineffective compared to the reliable gasoline used in peaceful times.

Once, Rolf untied the ropes, opened the door to the back compartment, and peered into the blackness.

"Everything's going fine," he said. "We're almost halfway. We've driven forty kilometers already. You can get out and stretch your legs if you want to. There's no one about."

"Someone could come suddenly," said Dr. Frænkel, inside in the dark. "We'll stay here, thanks."

Rolf could just make out where the Frænkels were sitting, with their backs against the wall, each one huddled on a box.

They looked like emigrants on the deck of a ship. He reached inside, caught hold of a hand. It was Miriam's.

"How cold you are. You're freezing!"

"No, I'm fine."

"You've changed places. Thought I had you behind me."

"Yes, I switched with Ole Jacob. I was afraid he'd be car-sick over there. It's less bumpy."

He warmed her hands. "Terje's stoking the generator."

A car came rushing around a corner. German military. Rolf slammed the door shut, flung himself into the front seat, where he sat like a whipped dog and waited. He heard Terje answering questions. Soon afterwards he climbed calmly in behind the wheel, and pressed the ignition switch.

"They wanted to know the way to Hauer Farm. Had trouble making myself sound like I knew my way around these parts. How should *I* know where Hauer Farm is . . . ?"

"What did you say?"

"I pointed west, because we're heading east."

They started up again, stopped a little farther ahead, and tied the doors open a crack so the refugees could get air. This time the car jerked. Terje had to get out and stoke the generator once more. Then they were off again, covering mileage on dark, back roads, the windshield wiper scraping back and forth, and grains of snow tumbling against the dark windshield. Terje felt hypnotized, as in a dream.

The boys changed places then. Rolf drove while Terje read directions. He had his own system of reading a map, Terje did. He gave short, confident orders at each cross road.

Rolf liked to drive. Then he had to concentrate on the driving so he could not think of the dangers Miriam and her family faced.

The snow gradually diminished. A sliver of a moon pushed through a wind-blown hole in the clouds, and shed a dim light on the road. Rolf increased his speed. An hour later they noticed that the wheel tracks were deep and full of holes as on an unpaved country road, and they realized they had made a wrong turn. Terje swore. "Stop here," he said.

Both boys jumped out, and saw a car which was standing in the shadow of the forest with its parking lights on.

"We'd better go over and ask where we are," said Terje. He wound his plaid scarf a few times around his neck and chin so as not to be recognizable. The boys stamped their feet on the frozen road to warm them. The wind had started to blow, and was whistling in the tree tops. A twig tumbled down and hit Rolf on the shoulder. Now the moon was hidden again.

"Talk about darkness. All I can see of that car is its parking lights. But there must be somebody inside. Somebody to ask." Terje knocked on the window. It was rolled down and a head thrust itself out.

Terje jumped back, gulped as though he had swallowed his own question and it had gone down his throat the wrong way. He grabbed Rolf by the elbow, and stumbled in the direction of the delivery truck.

"They're Germans! The same Germans!"

The boys jumped into their seats. Terje raced the motor and the car bumped along the road, which appeared to stop in a dead end in front of them.

"If only I could figure out how they got *there!*" Terje bent over the steering wheel, trying to avoid stones and holes. "And if only I could figure out how we got *here* . . ." He winced each time they went down into a deep rut. "Yes, I'm a fine one to be transporting refugees! Drive them straight into the woods, and park them right next to a German car! Shouldn't have taken on such a task . . ."

"Anyone can make a wrong turn in a place like this. In the middle of the night," comforted Rolf.

"That's just what's wrong. We should have been traveling in broad daylight, with forged passports. Day driving doesn't look half so mysterious as night driving."

That was Terje—one moment completely sure of himself, the next, in the depths of despair. Never anything in-between.

"But you insisted on driving at night," Rolf said. "I told you, remember . . ."

"Because the car is used by day. It would look strange if it were gone, and besides . . ." Now they were quarreling. Terje didn't stay remorseful for long when he was being contradicted.

Suddenly it seemed that a car with spotlights was behind them.

"Is it the Germans? Can you see?"

Rolf rolled down the window and leaned out. The sky was growing light. The road behind them was empty.

"No, they're probably waiting for daylight, so they can find their way out of that back road you directed them to."

"I wish we could get out ourselves. We don't have time for this fooling around."

Ten minutes later they were on the right road, just as inexplicably as they had been on the wrong one before. After a great deal of trouble, they also found the house in the forest to which they were going. Terje recognized it by the description he had been given and by certain significant signposts, understandable only to the initiated.

Rolf helped the three stiff-legged refugees out of the compartment. Ole Jacob had been sick inside the truck, and was feeling miserable.

It was now almost completely light. They entered a big room, which smelled of new lumber and wet boots. There were no curtains in front of the windows. Several men lay sleeping in their clothes on the benches.

The two boys and the Frænkels sat down at a table and waited for someone to wake up. No one noticed them. They ate the last remains of their provisions, though they were not very hungry.

Half an hour later Terje.turned the car around to drive back to Oslo. It was time to say goodbye. Miriam pressed her forehead against Rolf's shoulder.

"Look after Agda for me," she begged. "I hate the idea that she and Georg refused to come with us. Taking such a risk because of their new home and all their nice things!"

"They'll be all right," comforted Rolf. There were lots of

things he should have said to her, but it was impossible to do so now.

"Ugh, I dread going on." Miriam pointed in the direction of the thick forest which loomed on the far side of the clearing, half hidden by the morning mist. "Papa is too old for this sort of thing."

"Everything will be all right, you'll see," Rolf said. "You have first-class guides."

Then he kissed her. As the car drove off, he leaned out so as to watch Miriam for as long as he could see her. The three Frænkels waved. Miriam was wearing a woolen scarf knotted tightly under her chin, and a pair of rubber boots which were much too big for her. Ole Jacob was standing in exactly the same position as his father, looking like a smaller edition. Miriam could have made a funny drawing of the two, Rolf thought, and began to plan how he might get a job as a courier to Sweden or do something to be with Miriam again. He sat silent and unhappy.

As the truck swung out onto the main highway, another delivery truck slowed down. A boy leaned out of the window and asked directions to the clearing. Rolf recognized him at once. The boy was Arnt.

*   *   *   *   *

The two guides walked in front. Behind them, with a shapeless knapsack weighting him down, came Dr. Frænkel, and behind him, with short, quick steps, Mrs. Andresen, Arnt's mother. She was a tiny woman who wore large eyeglasses. She walked bent over against the wind as though she wanted to cleave her way through both the wind and the forest. She usually sat that way on the streetcar too, Miriam remembered—not leaning backwards or sitting upright as the other passengers did, but bent forwards as if to urge the streetcar ahead. Last in the procession walked Miriam and the two boys.

No one said a word.

They had spent the day waiting, while people came and went in the wooden house. For a time they had lain down and tried to sleep on the hard benches, while boots stamped in and out, and the woman of the house poured *ersatz* coffee from a pot which never seemed to empty, and packed sandwiches which would be their food until they reached Sweden.

Right after they had arrived, Arnt burst in on them, excited, restless, full of mischief. He was instantly best friends with Ole Jacob again, clapped him on the back, and told him about the night behind the woodpile, as if nothing had come between the two boys. And slowly Ole Jacob ventured out of his shell and was friends with Arnt again.

To Arnt, his present predicament was adventure. Away from school, away from lessons and chores, no office job for his mother any longer. Instead there was action, suspense, flight! But the day hadn't turned out the way he had imagined. The long waiting, and, afterwards, the slow tramping in snow and darkness and silence didn't suit Arnt's restless brain. He started bickering with his mother, and the guides had to speak to him.

The snow blew at them from the side, stinging their cheeks. The grains of snow struck the skin like tiny pin pricks. Everyone walked bent over a little, with the upper

part of the body twisted. After a few hours the group rested
by a pile of logs. Here the forest was thicker. The wind no
longer blew so fiercely though it whistled in the treetops
high above them. Now and then they caught sight of the
waning moon.

Miriam pulled off her boots and put a Band-aid on her
blisters. She was wearing Agda's boots, her own being too
small. The luminous hands on her watch told her that it
was midnight. She counted on her fingers. The refugees
were to arrive before daylight, so there couldn't be many
hours of walking left. How many, she didn't know, for she
couldn't remember when the days grew light at this time
of year, and she didn't want to ask. She looked at the boys.
They sat huddled in their windbreakers, as they chewed on
sandwiches, without uttering a word. Arnt was sulking. Beside them sat his mother. She looked as though she were
ready to jump up at the signal from the guide, and she
didn't eat. Miriam's father was rustling paper as he repacked
his knapsack, which was probably too heavy. When the
guides lit their pipes, Miriam saw that their faces were lined.
This surprised her. She had thought that mostly young men
were engaged in taking refugees across the border.

Soon the group started again and they walked for a couple
of hours. It seemed easier to walk after the rest. For a while
the group followed a well-beaten path, which made the
way seem shorter. One of the guides, who discovered that
Miriam was limping slightly, offered to carry her knapsack.
It was too small for him, and hung loosely over his left
shoulder, but he had to have his hands free, he said, in case

they ran into German patrols. The Germans usually had dogs with them, and the dogs had to be shot. You could get away from the Germans, if you knew your way around in the forest, but not from the dogs.

They had come out into trackless ground again, and now it was Arnt who was foot-sore. They rested again, the guides grumbling a little at the many stops, but they smoked while Mrs. Andresen pulled off Arnt's boots and patched up his heels. Miriam's Band-aid had rolled itself into a ball, making new blisters. Mrs. Andresen helped her tear off the old plaster and put on a new one. If only you could hop into Sweden on one leg, thought Miriam. But this forest was neither for hopping nor walking. Here were roots and stones to climb over and slopes to climb up. Miriam drank boiling hot coffee from the Thermos bottle, dried her wet face and looked hopefully into the thicket. They should be at least halfway. If only the guide hadn't talked about dogs! Now she was always imagining she heard barking, but if she stopped to listen, she realized that the sound was only the wind.

The next few hours were even harder. Miriam knew that if she stopped for a moment, she would fall asleep on her feet. She had to force herself ahead over the uneven ground. The temptation to sit down for only half a minute was almost impossible to resist. But suddenly she was wide awake. The guides cautioned them to go silently, for here there was danger of patrols. So they walked on tiptoe, lifted their tired legs over dry branches and twigs, and hushed one another excitedly. And fear made them forget their exhaustion for a while. Arnt, fully roused, scouted with alert eyes into the darkness. And again it seemed to Miriam that she could hear barking far away, but decided she imagined it.

*   *   *   *   *

At last they were standing on the top of a barren ridge, looking down. It wasn't completely dark, a sliver of a moon shone whitely on a lake below. They were told that half of it lay in Sweden. They had only to go down there, follow along the shore, and report at the very first house they came to. The guides said goodbye. They were no longer needed, and had to make use of the darkness to return safely through the most dangerous part of the forest.

Miriam lifted her knapsack onto her shoulders again. She watched the two silent guides as they disappeared into the forest. She wanted to shout after them to return. She felt as if they were taking with them all security and help as they went. Her father looked as if he felt the same way as he stared near-sightedly down at the moonlit lake and figured out the distance.

The lake seemed close, but as soon as the group had reached the other side of the ridge, the moon disappeared behind a cloud and a new ridge hid the water. When they got to the top, they saw only forest.

The boys had fallen back to the rear, and suddenly they started to quarrel. Ole Jacob didn't understand how it began. He had been unbelievably happy the whole day because he and Arnt were friends again. Arnt hadn't meant the nasty thing he'd said. It was only his way of trying to make some-one angry, the same way he stuck the pin in the frog to see it hop. But he didn't *mean* to be nasty.

And then all at once they were enemies again. Arnt had uttered an oath because of the blister, Ole Jacob remembered afterwards. And he also remembered that he, Ole Jacob, had said something to the effect that if Miriam, who was a girl, could walk with blisters on her feet, then Arnt certainly ought to manage too. And suddenly came the words which made everything fall apart.

Arnt didn't whisper them, he shrieked: "You ought to mind your own business, *you* who turned in your friends . . . I saw you all right!"

"Turned in?" Ole Jacob was yelling just as loudly as Arnt. "What do you mean, 'turned in'?"

"Don't you think I saw when you were running with those German soldiers? That day Goebbels came to Oslo. When Rolf and Terje were taken. You're the one who pointed them out. I saw you all right!"

And because of the startling effect he had produced the first time, he added: "You're not Norwegian!"

What happened next came so fast that no one was able to stop it. The boys were at each other's throats, didn't even have time to throw down their knapsacks. They wrestled in the darkness and rolled over and over right off the edge of a cliff. When the others got to them, Arnt lay groaning. Ole Jacob was standing, his whole body trembling with anger, with exhaustion, with fright over what had happened.

Dr. Frænkel loosened Arnt's clothing and examined him. His mother bent over him, crying. She turned a knapsack upside down, emptied out the contents, found a flashlight and shone it on Arnt's arms and legs. Ole Jacob was bleed-

ing from a cut on his mouth, but on Arnt not a broken bone
or a scratch was to be found. He had hit his chest against
a root in his fall, and had the wind knocked out of him.
For a time, he wasn't able to speak. He could only groan.

They sat around Arnt while his mother gave him a drink
from a Thermos.

"I'll carry him," said Dr. Fraenkel, when Arnt's breathing
was calmer. "We're almost there now." He put down his
knapsack.

"No," said Arnt, suddenly able to speak when he feared
Ole Jacob's father would lift him up. "I want to walk by
myself."

Ole Jacob sighed with relief. Arnt had spoken in his usual
voice so then he couldn't be badly hurt. Ole Jacob whispered to his father:

"I'm sorry, Papa. Sorry I flew at Arnt."

"So am I. As if refugees didn't have enough to do to keep
together." He spoke severely. "What did he say to you that
made you so angry?"

"He said . . . Oh, it doesn't matter." Ole Jacob's voice
was weary. His anger had left him when he thought he had
broken his comrade's back. But humiliation itself remained
like a thorn, pushed in so deeply that no one could reach it.

"What are we going to do about it, Papa, that we're Jews,
I mean?" He looked up at his father's face without really
seeing it clearly in the darkness.

"Do about it? Why nothing, of course. You're to be proud
of it."

"Yes, I know. But people seem to think it's wrong of us to be Jews."

His father didn't answer, only put his hand on his son's shoulder as if he wanted to protect the boy but couldn't.

"We'll talk more about this when we reach Sweden, my boy."

Dr. Frænkel went over to Arnt.

"How are you?"

"He's much better," said his mother. "We can certainly go on now."

"Then the two of you had better make peace and shake hands," said Dr. Frænkel to the boys. "Arnt, you've hurt Ole Jacob's feelings and he's injured you. Now you're even."

Hesitatingly the boys shook hands. Both were glad for the darkness.

And now Mrs. Andresen discovered that she had lost her glasses, probably when she had slid down the cliff after the boys. Everyone helped search for the glasses with flashlight and matches, but did not find them.

"It can't be helped. I can get new ones in Sweden," she said. "If only we knew where Sweden was," she added with a sigh. She had eaten little the whole day, and the shock had exhausted her. She was growing weak.

They seemed now to have lost their sense of direction completely. Some of the group wanted to go to the right, others to the left. The moon had disappeared behind a cloud again. They walked on, mostly by guesswork. Mrs. Andresen put her arm around Arnt's shoulders, for without glasses she could hardly see. They plodded up and down stony ridges for half an hour longer. There was no path, and walking was difficult.

"This is wrong," said Dr. Frænkel. "It wasn't such a long way to the lake. Sit here, all of you, while I get my bearings." He put down his knapsack.

"Papa, may I come with you?" It was Ole Jacob who touched his hand in the darkness. "You know, if I hadn't flown at Arnt, we'd probably have been at the lake by now."

"I don't think so," said Dr. Frænkel. "But it must be nearby. You stay here and make sure that no one falls asleep."

"All right, Papa."

They heard him tramp into the forest. Dry branches and twigs crackled under his feet with every step.

It was good to throw off the knapsacks for a while. The group sat on them while they waited. Never had they known what *real* fatigue was before now. Ole Jacob was aware of Mrs. Andresen sitting beside him, upright against a tree trunk. He shook her.

"It's dangerous to fall asleep!"

She immediately leaned forward again, the way she usually did. A little later something hard and cold struck him in the face. He himself had drowsed and had slumped down into the new snow. With difficulty he arose—his body heavy and weary. He turned to talk to the others. Hadn't his father said no one must fall asleep? Did he say it today? Or was it yesterday?

But Ole Jacob didn't have to wake anyone. They were all jumping to their feet as a terrifying sound of barking filled the air. No imagination this time. Somewhere in the forest dogs barked and above the barking rasped the shout of commands.

"Papa!" cried Miriam. "They'll get Papa!"

She turned, started running in the direction of the commotion. "We must help him. He's so impractical, he'll never make it! We must help him!" She stumbled over a root and fell.

Ole Jacob pulled her to her feet. "The dogs!" he shouted. "They're coming this way! We must run!"

Beside themselves with fear, the four of them ran for their lives. Blindly they plunged on, hopped over stones, tore through thickets. Their knapsacks were left behind. Five knapsacks standing in a ring in the underbrush.

Suddenly they were by the lake. It stretched out ahead of them in the gray light of morning, a long, snow-covered surface which ended in freedom, somewhere in the fog. It was almost completely light. They had followed the shore for a long time without noticing it. Behind them someone was shouting at dogs.

They started running again, but the barking was far away.

"They've caught Papa," cried Miriam.

"Yes, they've caught Papa," said Ole Jacob, who was too tired and confused to feel anything.

Down by the shore stood a cottage. There were lights in the windows and smoke was rising from the chimney. People were up.

"Maybe it's a German sentry-post," said Mrs. Andresen. "Why, we don't even know if we're in Norway or Sweden!"

She squinted in the direction of the house, unable to see well without her glasses.

Miriam slumped down onto the ground. She didn't care where they were. Nothing mattered now that Papa had been caught.

Mrs. Andresen and Arnt walked up to the cottage. She still had her arm around her son's shoulders. As the two stepped on to the porch, the door opened and a woman came out.

"Are you Norwegian?" she asked.

They were in Sweden.

11 *AGDA*

Hanne missed Miriam. She missed their stolen moments up in the attic, the outings on Sundays, their talks and secrets. Nonetheless, she was glad she was gone. A week after the drive to the clearing, the great hunt for Norwegian Jews began.

Until then the drive hadn't been organized, and it was not too risky for Norwegians to meet and talk with Jews. The Nazis in Norway evidently had other things to think of. But suddenly there came new orders from Berlin, and on a dark November night all Jewish houses were raided and all males including fifteen-year-old boys were arrested.

A deep gloom lay over the city. People tried to protect the Jews, however dangerous it had become to do so. A nursing home for Jewish refugee children was emptied right under the noses of the Gestapo, and the children smuggled into Sweden. People took food and clothing from their own meager rations and sent them to the collection depots. From there the packages went twice a week to Berg concentration camp where the Jews starved and froze.

At the factory it was rumored that Dr. Frænkel had been captured by the Germans right at the Swedish border, and sent to Berg Concentration Camp, too.

It was then that Hanne started taking packages to the collection depots. There was nothing else she could do now for Miriam. With her mother Hanne buttered many large sandwiches and delivered them promptly. On package days people tramped in and out of the depots—Jews and Gentiles alike. Once Hanne saw Mrs. Kjeldsen with a big bundle. In the tiny apartment, which served as a collection depot, strange wares piled up along the walls and on the floor. The two small rooms were as dirty as a sidewalk. Weeping girls and old women opened and re-packed, opened and re-packed, making sure that no forbidden articles or messages were hidden in the parcels.

One day Hanne ran into Agda. She had changed and wasn't as pretty as she had been. Her self-confidence was gone. With her coat unbuttoned, she sat on a packing case and put sandwiches in a paper carton, as if she were too tired to stand up and work. At first Hanne couldn't believe that this untidy young woman, with her unkempt hair falling halfway down her back, could be Agda. Agda, who had been so pretty, who was always ready with a joke . . . no, it was impossible.

But it was Agda all the same. She stood up when she caught sight of Hanne.

"Hello," she said.

"Hello," Hanne answered. The greeting sounded strangely commonplace here, where everything was so tragic and solemn, where people cried without even trying to hide their tears.

Agda brushed up a tuft of hair and fastened it with a hairpin. "All the curl has gone out of my hair, but I don't dare sit under a hairdryer now. Then both the machine and I would be arrested." She laughed a little, and Hanne understood that Agda was talking about her hair to keep from having to talk about Georg who was at Berg Concentration Camp.

"You know they pray for us in the churches all over the country," Agda whispered as if she were surrounded by enemies even here in this friendly, untidy little room.

Hanne nodded.

"Brave of them," Agda sighed, as if she meant it would do more harm to the pastors than good to the Jews. And she probably was right about that.

"Miriam?" asked Hanne quietly.

"She and Ole Jacob are safe in Sweden, but Papa is at Berg," said Agda, and now the tears flowed, and were wiped away by a handkerchief that was still wet from previous weeping.

Hanne wanted to hug her, to comfort her, but it is difficult to comfort someone across a carton of sandwiches. "Go and join them in Sweden," she whispered.

Agda shook her head. "That's what Rolf wanted me to do, too. But how can I leave Georg and Papa? Who knows, maybe they'll get very sick, so sick that they'll have to be put in a hospital where I can visit them. Things do turn out well sometimes . . ."

That was the last time Hanne saw Agda. Hanne always remembered her standing there, surrounded by packages for the prison, wishing for her loved ones, weeping, and holding onto her own elbows. She had nothing else to hold onto. A week later she was arrested, and with hundreds of others was sent on the long trek, which so many had to journey, and from which so few returned.

* * * * *

At Christmas Hanne received a letter from Miriam. Hanne smiled when she saw that Miriam had chosen the name "Inger Rasmussen" as sender, the name which had popped into Hanne's mind on that terrible evening, when things had nearly gone wrong for Miriam, too.

The letter came from an address in Stockholm:

Dear Hanne!

Your old cousin Inger wishes you a Merry Christmas. We are all well here. Everyone is kind to us. Rolf writes and says he is going to be a painter. When I read his letters I have such an aching desire to be with him again, take walks with him, run hand in hand with him down steep hills, the way we did at home when we were in good spirits. Here, nothing really matters.

In many ways we are much better off than in those two small, narrow, disorderly rooms, but I'm so terribly home-sick. Yes, I even miss the "Katzenjammer Kids," and I never thought I'd do that.

I've been in the hospital for a while with an impossible leg; got blood poisoning from a blister. But now I'm fine again. My brother—(she had first written his name, but crossed it out carefully again)—is unbelievably smart at school. Can you remember how lazy he was before? Now he'll soon be the smartest one in the class, but I almost liked him better as he was. Back home we always thought the war would be over by Christmas or Easter, but here they think it will take years.

Almost at the end of the letter, as though she wanted to forget the question, there came:

Do you hear anything of Papa? I thought maybe the factory or your father might be able to tell me a little. He's so forgetful about writing, himself. And do you know the least bit about A and G?

"Oh! If only someone did have something to tell "Inger"! But Hanne had heard nothing about A and G, or "Inger's" father. Nothing more than that the town was seething with bitterness at the way the Jews had been treated, but was helpless to protect them. And she didn't know when the war would end either.

The letter went on to say that Miriam was attending art classes at night and working in the daytime. It ended with more Christmas greetings:

> *In five days it will be Christmas at home. Maybe you've already bought your Christmas tree, and have it standing outside the house, between the kitchen door and the old woodshed, until time for decoration. O.J. sends greetings. He has a cold, but will have his tonsils out in the spring. Merry Christmas, and write!*

> *Your*
Inger.

12 *ENCOUNTER IN STOCKHOLM*

One cold Sunday morning, on a street in Stockholm, Rolf ran into Miriam. He was on leave from a military camp in Sweden, close to the border, where he was being trained as a saboteur. He had to be back and in uniform the next day and since the Legation closed early on Saturdays, he had been unable to inquire for Miriam's address, but had spent the previous evening searching for her in the suburbs. Now he was strolling along the sidewalk, scanning passers-by. He had almost passed Miriam without recognizing her when suddenly he was aware of her narrow gray eyes, her straight brows, and dark hair, and knew it could be no one else.

He turned quickly and saw that she had stopped and was coming back.

"Miriam! So I did find you after all."

"Rolf!" She stared at him as though she didn't trust her own eyes, or wasn't sure whether he had changed and become a stranger since that night so long ago when they had to say goodbye.

"Miriam," he said again, standing with her hand in his, unable to say another word.

Two and a half long years had gone by. Two and a half hard years, crammed with underground activities, with shocks and dangers. He had never stopped thinking of her in all that time. Faintly he remembered girls he had met in those hectic years when death was just around the corner. Now, as he stood here with Miriam's hand in his, he knew no other girl could ever take her place.

As in the past, he admired the dark, small head set so proudly! She might be an exiled princess, he thought. Until this moment he had not realized how deeply he cared for her—but then he had been a mere boy when she had left!

"I had the maddest idea about running away to Sweden to find you." Speech came back to him at last, and from then on he couldn't stop talking: "But there was always some new mission in the underground, and, as you know, Norway has become a prison. Nobody is allowed to go to Sweden just because he is in love. You can't leave even illegally unless you get permission from the underground *and* an escort."

"I know, Rolf. And if you leave without an escort you

run into the arms of the Germans. I'm glad you didn't try *that*."

"Why did we ever stop writing, Miriam?"

She smiled. "Well, you'll have to answer that question yourself."

"And then you moved. How on earth could you think of moving?"

Now he remembered how merrily her gray eyes twinkled when she laughed. Serious girls are pretty when they laugh.

"I did send you my new address."

"You did?" He felt relieved as though she had said: "I have by no means forgotten you."—"But you see, I haven't had a home address for ages, not even my own name. No letter could find me, only orders."

A dark boy of fourteen, lingering in the background, slowly approached.

"Bother," Rolf thought. "Ole Jacob is here too. Of course he would be."

Ole Jacob tried to smile. There he stood in a winter coat with sleeves a little too short, a very dark, foreign-looking boy, smiling up at his old ideal Rolf! Rolf himself, who once, long ago, had put Arnt in his place, and saved Ole Jacob's honor as a Norwegian!

Rolf couldn't bear to disappoint that eager face. He let go of Miriam's hand and turned to her brother.

"Ole Jacob! The voice of Norway! I didn't recognize you, lad."

"Hello Rolf, how have you been all this time?" His voice was changing and unexpectedly switched over to a childish discord. He was wearing glasses and looked as though he was reading too much.

"I'm fine. And you? Seem to be all right too." Rolf went on agreeably despite his one desire to be alone with Miriam.

"I'm all right. Especially now that I've met a countryman." Ole Jacob smiled happily.

"How long will you be here?" Miriam asked. That was the most one could permit oneself to ask a Norwegian one met in Stockholm.

"Have to be back tomorrow. My two-day pass is considered a minor miracle."

Now Miriam knew that Rolf was in the Norwegian police troops. She asked no more questions.

"And you, Miriam? What are you doing?" Rolf put his arm around her shoulders.

"I'm going to art classes in the evening, and I have a job during the day."

What sweet little shoulders she had! He remembered a summer day, when he'd sat and held his arm around them and comforted her. Yes, it all came back to him now so clearly, standing here on a sidewalk in Stockholm, that he could almost smell the scent of pine needles and warm forest-ground as it was that day.

People bumped into them. They were in the way on this busy Stockholm sidewalk. And if they walked three abreast, they would still be in the way.

"Let's go somewhere and have some cakes," suggested Rolf, without stopping to think that he was pleasing himself more with this suggestion than the others.

"Yes, let's go somewhere where we can talk," said Miriam.

It had been snowing in Stockholm that morning and the late spring snow had been trampled into slush by Sunday promenading feet. The group found a large well-heated tea-room—where there were more cakes than customers—and sat down at a table by the window. As the day was still early, empty tables and chairs surrounded them on all sides.

No matter how they have fared otherwise, at least they have had plenty to eat, thought Rolf, comparing their plates with his own over-loaded one. Having arrived from an oc-cupied country, he still had the newcomer's unsatisfied appetite.

"Ole Jacob, I just want to tell you that there are real almonds in these macaroons. Not 'ersatz' ones. Don't you want a couple?"

"Thanks! A thousand thanks, I already had one," said Ole Jacob. He was indifferent to these delicacies. For two years cakes had been a great solace for them since they were cheap and within the means even of refugees. They had eaten pastries when they were near despair—and it had helped somewhat. *"You* take some. You ought to put on weight. You're so bony."

"Now let's hear a little about you." Rolf turned to Miriam, finding his own undernourished appearance a dull topic. "I know so little about you. All the letters I did receive were censored, of course, and I'm not clever at reading between the lines . . . Or writing that way."

Miriam had to smile. She remembered his letters—full of

weather and small news. And that he was just fine which she guessed was rather untrue.

"Oh Rolf, it's so good to see you! You know I almost feel a little shy. You're huge. Even bigger than I remembered."

He ran brown fingers through his hair. "Shy!—That I won't stand for. There's not a girl I feel so much at home with as I do with you. Just because I'm two years older and bigger shouldn't make you shy!"

"You're right. Real friendship doesn't change, no matter how big one grows."

To conceal her happiness, she turned her head and looked out at the snow and the crowds hurrying past. It was funny about Rolf—clumsy in many ways. She still remembered how he stepped on her toes when they danced. But he had his own nice way of saying things, to make one happy . . . In this way, at any rate, he wasn't clumsy.

She loosened her scarf and let it fall around her shoulders. "Tell me about Hanne. And Terje, of course."

Now he noticed fondly how her hair still curled about her forehead. That she had changed, of course, was to be expected after two and a half years. The sports jacket was too tight and made her appear different from the well-dressed young girls in the city. Her tiny face was even prettier than he recalled—more like her sister's now. Her youthful body was no longer thin and slouchy but firm and supple. She was lovely.

"Terje, you said . . . well he . . . why yes, he's doing excellent work. Hanne is in the Underground too. Things have started to move now. Lots to do."

Ole Jacob leaned eagerly across the table.

"Oh Rolf! Can't . . . couldn't we go somewhere where you could tell us more about your work and . . ."

"I'm afraid not." Rolf shook his head, smiling ruefully at the disappointed boy. "Not that you're not trustworthy. Not that there is much chance of the Gestapo getting hold of you in *this* country. But our orders are to tell no one anything —it makes our task desperately difficult sometimes. . . ."

"How lucky you are!" Miriam sighed. "If only I could be home now and do something useful instead of just earning money for food."

She had an expression on her face which he knew well —a look that meant she was disturbed or lonely or tired. As so often before, when he was with her, he was reminded —strangely enough—of something from his childhood, the old pin cushion which used to stand on his mother's sewing table. It was red and shaped like a heart, and that was what made it so interesting and curious for him. When he was quite small he had stood now and then and watched the pin cushion receiving needles and pins, thick and thin, one after the other, and he had always thought that the thinnest needles must hurt the most. Now that silly pin cushion had popped into his head again. Idiotic comparison. Miriam's heart did not in the least resemble that old pin cushion. But think of all the hard blows it had received already! And the deep unpleasant jabs.

He started talking about something which would make her smile. Not a word about Hanne traveling with weapons

from town to town, only of her more peaceful activities in-
between.

"Hanne is attending Business College now. She wants to
get a job when the war is over and earn a lot of money so
that she can afford to marry Terje."

Miriam laughed. If only he could make her laugh oftener,
he thought. She was so sweet when she laughed.

"Hanne will certainly manage to support a whole family!"

"Yes indeed. Terje is in good hands. As a matter of fact,
we were in hiding together last week. Can you guess where?"

"I give up. I'm no good at riddles."

"At Miss Lepsoe's. That seamstress you used to go to."

Miriam remembered a green woolen dress she had never
worn, a bright new dress which now lay rotting in a knapsack on the Swedish border.

"Miss Lepsoe? But all she has is a narrow little dining
room."

"Oh no. She has also a big living room for company which
she had never heated. But she heated it for *us*. There were
three of us who lay there for fourteen days."

"I remember she called Goebbels a nasty Jew." Miriam
smiled. Now she could think the remark humorous.

"Goebbels of all people!"

So there were pin pricks that had healed, thought Rolf.

"She had Jews in hiding, too. People don't always mean
the queer things they say, or understand what they are saying sometimes. Miss Lepsoe is all right. 'The aunt of the
Home Front' we call her. But you say so little about yourself.
How are you getting along?"

"Fine, more or less. My drawing is improving, and I have a good job in a flower shop. Do you have a cigarette?"

"Certainly." Rolf took out a pack. It was empty.

"I'll go and buy some," said Ole Jacob. His voice broke again, and blushing, he glanced at Rolf reproachfully, as if he were to blame. Ole Jacob blushed easily as lonely children tend to do. Miriam shook her head.

"Being away from Norway is worst for Ole Jacob," she said after he had gone. "He reads himself half to death and I can't stop him. And he's become so touchy."

Rolf watched her with concern. He had an idea that she constantly concealed her anxiety but that the slightest incident might break her reserve and reveal her sorrow. He tried to reassure her about Ole Jacob.

"Oh he has always been sensitive." Rolf tried to comfort her. "You remember Arnt, the trouble-maker, who made him run wild with his silly remarks?" He moved his chair close to hers, took her hand and kissed it. But still Miriam's eyes were full of sadness.

"No courage now," she said. "As a matter of fact we have all become a little queer, living as refugees for such a long time. Some days we are mad at everybody and everything, even at the landscape because it isn't up and down and full of hills, at the Swedes because they're not Norwegians, at Sweden because it is neutral—even though its neutrality has saved us. They've been wonderful to us—the Swedes."

He ought to inquire about her family now but somehow could not do it. Miriam was the one to ask about his instead.

"And your parents? How are they?"

"So-so," he told her. "Living in a rooming house and hating it. Our house was confiscated by Gestapo officials."

"Oh, that pretty, pretty house."

"Mother, poor thing, really feels the loss most. She has little to do. Only herself to concentrate on, like a cog-wheel with nothing to put its teeth into. And now she hasn't even got me to take spots off of." He glanced down at his gray tweed Swedish overcoat that he had just bought. It was unbelievably new and spotless.

When Ole Jacob returned with the cigarettes, he had wet snow in his hair, on his coat, and even on his eyelashes. Rolf pulled his chair very close to Miriam's, lit her cigarette and watched her sketch on a piece of paper.

"Too bad I have to be back tomorrow," Rolf said.

Miriam looked up at him and smiled sadly, then went on drawing. Ole Jacob sat down, straddling the chair with his arms along the back.

"Now the war's going so well on all fronts, you two will soon be together again." Rolf remembered that Ole Jacob had a way of tossing out words of comfort to no one in particular.

"Funny, but we are almost dreading the peace, Ole Jacob and I," said Miriam. "It still seems as though everything is hidden behind a huge curtain, just as at the theater. And as long as that curtain is there, we're allowed to believe and hope what we like. Can you understand that we are dreading the peace?"

Now he could see that she was drawing her father. There

was no mistaking that big, angular face with glasses. She didn't mention him, only sketched him.

"Tell us something exciting, Rolf," said Ole Jacob.

Obligingly, Rolf spoke about the camp on the Swedish border, about fuses and dynamite and learning to blow bridges sky-high and camouflage and a face covered with soot. Strange that these should be subjects which seemed now both good and safe. Ole Jacob stared in fascination. Soon, he guessed, Rolf would be ordered across the border to blow up bridges and otherwise annoy the enemy . . . and soon he would meet the allied soldiers and help in liberating his country. How Ole Jacob envied Rolf. Ole Jacob knew he ought to leave . . . that Rolf and Miriam probably wished to be alone, but somehow the time went by and Ole Jacob still stayed, reluctant to go.

In the evening Rolf and Miriam went to the Opera. They sat in the dark holding hands, not listening too attentively to the lovely music which swept over them. They prowled through the streets in the worst drizzle Rolf could remember. Everything was closed when they left the restaurant where they had dined. It was too cold to sit down, too cold to stand still. Soon his shoes were soaked through but every time they came to Miriam's front door, and said goodnight, he put his coat around her again, and they walked around the block once more until the streets had become quite empty in the night. It had taken hours for her to unburden herself of all her sorrows and worries which suddenly broke loose after having been controlled all day. It took Rolf all those hours to comfort her and renew her courage.

Perhaps all the kisses he gave her that evening pushed the thoughts of her father and Agda into the background for a while. Never had he kissed a girl like that before. Never had he felt such an overwhelming desire to *protect* someone. He wanted to take her in his arms, and carry her far away where no evil could reach her. She must have felt his love and compassion for in the end she became still and happy. Before he let her go, she was as sweet and lively as in the old days, and her face was no longer wet with tears. Only with rain.

13 *PEACE*

Germany had surrendered. From the second it was known, Stockholm became a wild scene of dancing, jubilant, laughing people. On the way home from school, which had closed at once for the day, Ole Jacob was embraced three times by strangers, just because he was wearing a Norwegian flag on his jacket. From a window, a basketful of paper was emptied over his head, and suddenly from every window, shreds of paper floated through the air. The Carnival of Peace had broken loose.

In Norway, however, the Germans still held out, but

everyone assured Ole Jacob that they would soon give up, certainly by tomorrow, or the next day, or the day after that. Outside the flower shop where Miriam worked, he ran into her, and together they rushed up one street and down the next. Suddenly, they were friends with the whole world. They had thousands of friends, most of whom were out on the streets, and all were happy.

"Soon we will be home again! Soon! Soon!" shouted Ole Jacob for joy. He had wound a long paper streamer around his neck. Infected with the high spirits around him he had for the moment not a care in the world. They would be home again—he and Miriam. They would live at "The Old Court." Oslo would be swept clean of Nazi uniforms.

Someone grabbed his hand and suddenly he and Miriam were torn along in a snake dance of young people who were laughing and singing. A Danish boy pulled Miriam out of the line and over to the edge of the sidewalk, where cars inched by, honking. He had heard her Norwegian accent and just wanted to reassure her that Norway would soon be free.

"Tomorrow at the very latest!" he declared. "They said so up at the Embassy, too! You've got to look happy! Everybody's happy today."

He himself was perspiring from happiness. Sometime afterwards Miriam saw him sitting on the back of a truck, waving an empty box over his head.

Miriam put in her appearance at Aug. Lindgreen's Flower Shop two hours late, and had a guilty conscience because she had been dancing in the streets instead of reporting for a new round of deliveries. But here, too, everyone was hanging out of the windows, and with his own hands Mr. Lindgreen pinned a bunch of daisies on her uniform.

"Soon we'll be losing Miriam. Congratulations all the same!" he said.

Miriam had enough to keep her busy in the days to come. She was a messenger girl for a large flower shop, with a sizable clientele, and in these days of rejoicing, everyone sent flowers—a flood of them seemingly. Then, three days later, when the Germans surrendered in Norway, there was such a fresh wave of congratulations that Miriam almost collapsed in the rush of deliveries. Never had she imagined that so many bouquets and so many flights of stairs could be found in the whole world.

Not that she complained. The messenger girls at Aug. Lindgreen and Co. were better off than most. A large green delivery truck, with a chauffeur in green-and-gold uniform, drove them whenever they had long distances to go. The messenger girl in most instances was expected to run up stairs, ring doorbells, wait on thresholds for someone to receive the flowers, and to look sweet and appealing in a green pleated skirt and a gold-trimmed bellboy cap.

Lindgreen selected his messenger girls with care. Often he chose them for their smiles, not just for their attractive legs and figures. "A messenger girl must complement the flowers," he said. "Everyone likes to receive flowers from a nice girl."

Miriam went about in a daze. Her head swam from exhaustion and happiness, and hopes and anxiety. She would drop by the Refugee Office, no matter how busy she was, hoping for news of her father and Agda. Prince Bernadotte of Sweden, the president of the Red Cross, had sent his white cars to German concentration camps to fill them with Danish and Norwegian prisoners. There were eighty big, white buses which collectively could hold thousands of the released prisoners. They couldn't be expected back for some time, but lists with names of the survivors had already been telegraphed.

For Miriam and Ole Jacob, there was still no news—no official bulletins, no reports containing the names she was hunting. There were no letters or telegrams . . . only rumors. At the shop everyone was solicitous in a peculiar way, that chilled more than comforted her.

A few weeks after the surrender, she and Carlsson, the chauffeur, were making deliveries to a Stockholm suburb. The green truck was full of bouquets arranged in piles. Miriam was feeling the old injury to her left leg, the one that had become infected on the flight across the border more than two years ago. The last hectic days of running up and down stairs had started the aching again. And Carlsson, who saw that she was limping, helpfully carried a pile of wreaths into a mortuary chapel.

"When Miriam gets home, Miriam must put her leg up on a chair." Carlsson's polite Swedish manners were mingled with sympathy. "Or else Miriam will be out of a job."

Miriam replied that when she got home she had to do the marketing and fix dinner for herself and her brother.

"We'll stop here and do the marketing now," said Carlsson.

"And then you'll let the boy fix dinner. Miriam must be a little practical."

He pulled up in front of a grocery store so that Miriam could make her purchases. Carlsson was kind. In her confusion lately, she had made a few mistakes, delivered bouquets to wrong addresses. Carlsson had helped straighten out her errors.

Now there was only one bouquet left for a place in the outskirts of Stockholm. It was a rooming house for refugees where several Norwegians lived.

The truck parked before a high, four-story building, with white lace curtains on small windows. Miriam rang the bell, and the door was opened by a boy of fourteen. Involuntarily she drew back, the way she had done long ago, on her sixteenth birthday, when she had been frightened by a face in the window. The boy who stood there now was Arnt. At second glance, he didn't look formidable. In fact, he appeared ill at ease.

"Is it you?" he asked, to have something to say. She did not believe he was happy to see her. He had changed and seemed calmer, as though the years had given him time to reflect. His face was pale and full of pimples. He asked, "How's Ole Jacob?"

"Fine, thanks," said Miriam a little shortly. The boys had avoided one another ever since that night at the border, and even though Ole Jacob had never mentioned the reason for the fight, Miriam had guessed much of it.

Arnt stood looking down. "I'm sorry your father's dead," he said.

"He's not dead!" Miriam cried harshly.

Arnt did not listen.

"I know it's my fault," he said. "Mother claims it was Ole Jacob's fault, because he flew at me, but he wouldn't have been angry if I hadn't . . . I shouldn't have said what I did there in the forest." He glanced up and away. "But how was I to know that it would turn out like that? That your father would die?"

"He's not dead, do you hear!"

"Isn't he? But everyone says he is. Have you heard from him?" Arnt suddenly had hope. If Ole Jacob's father were alive, then he, Arnt, needn't go around thinking of the bad part he had played, needn't dream about it at night, imagining himself pursued by dogs and soldiers. "Have you heard from him?" he repeated.

"He is not dead," said Miriam emphatically. "Don't you dare say he's dead! He's alive, he *must* be alive!"

All the old bitterness against this boy welled up in her. She couldn't bear to look at him any longer. Turning her back on him, she ran quickly down the flagstones towards the sidewalk.

"But have you heard anything of him?" Arnt raced after her. "He isn't with any of the Bernadotte cars!"

She didn't reply.

"The flowers," he said meekly. "Weren't you supposed to deliver the flowers?"

Miriam came to her senses. She mustn't make any more mistakes now, just because she wasn't able to collect her thoughts. She handed him the bouquet. "Will you please deliver them for me?" she said in quite another voice. "In the rooming house. No, of course I'm not angry with you. It was only an accident. A terrible accident."

Arnt took the flowers and walked slowly up the steps to the rooming house.

"Well, now Miriam is sick," said Carlsson when he saw how pale she was. "Now I'm going to drive Miriam straight home. Where does Miriam live?"

Miriam told him her address, leaned her head back, and closed her eyes. She was a little nauseated. Otherwise she felt nothing during this trip but gratitude for Carlsson.

With her grocery bag under her arm, she walked up the five flights to the two-room apartment where she and Ole Jacob lived, and let herself in.

Rolf, she thought, remembering his handsome face and how he had looked at her. If only Rolf were here. He knew how to say things which made her happy, but soon there wouldn't be anything left in the whole world that could make her happy.

As she set down the bag of groceries, she saw a letter lying on the table and she knew that now she would find out. But when she tried to open the envelope, her hand shook so much that she had to put it down again, as though it were too heavy to hold. Twice she walked around the table and looked at the large, pale envelope, with the typewritten address. Only when she heard Ole Jacob on the stairs did she seize it in a panic. He must not know . . . not just yet . . .

he must find out in a nicer way . . . She ran into her room, locked the door, sat down on the edge of the bed and opened the envelope.

Dear Miriam,

The factory has been told not to expect your father back any more. First the director wanted to send you a telegram, and asked us for your address, but I persuaded him to let me write instead, because I think it hurts a little less for you and Ole Jacob to hear about them from a friend, I mean. They have been dead for over a year, all three of them. And now I have said it.

Dear, sweet Miriam. You must come home to us at once. Ole Jacob too. You must live with us. Live at "The Old Court," which is your home, your furniture. Yes, for we are the only family you have now. Pack your suitcase and come. I'll go down and meet every single train from to-morrow on.

When you come, we'll cry together, it's so dreadful to cry alone.

Your
Hanne.

14 *NOT JUST PEACE*

"The Old Court" looked just as big and gray and shabby as before. But Miriam and Ole Jacob knew they would rather live there than anywhere else in the world.

At the factory a memorial service was held for Dr. Fræn-kel. The director and many others said many kind words about him—how brilliant he had been . . . how he would be missed. Then the director shook Miriam and Ole Jacob by the hand, and patted them on the cheek, and told them they mustn't worry about the future. It would be taken care of for them, and they could live in "The Old Court" as long as they wished.

Miriam wasn't worried about anything. On the contrary, she was indifferent. From the moment she read Hanne's letter, she had stiffened into an unmelting composure. She wanted to get rid of that composure, because it hurt to go about with a clump of ice inside, but she remained numb and frozen.

The director, who saw Miriam's unmoving face, and knew of her artistic talents, had managed to get her admitted to the Art Academy. As a special favor, she was allowed to begin in the modeling class at once, instead of having to wait until the Fall term. And Miriam, who in the past would have considered this a glorious dream come true, now felt only a weary gratitude to the director. Before beginning her first project she stood for some moments with the cold clay between her fingers, then slowly started shaping her father's face.

The days passed. The garden's two apple trees were in full bloom, but already the petals had begun to fall, drifting like snow flakes from the twisted branches. Ole Jacob had started school. Rolf was stationed with his army troop in northern Norway.

The day the letter arrived announcing that Rolf had been given leave, and was arriving by military plane, Hanne breathed easier. But Miriam showed no real joy then, either. She sat up in the attic room, which she now shared with Hanne, and appeared barely to listen to her friend. Hanne walked back and forth and talked. She had made up her mind that she would do what she could to keep Miriam from brooding. So Hanne spoke of the last, hectic days in the underground movement, when she traveled with money and weapons to the towns in the south of Norway. She and Terje had become engaged at this time. They had both insisted on a real, old-fashioned engagement, with a ring and everything.

"We decided not to wait," said Hanne, throwing out her arms. "Because we never knew if we'd be alive the next day."

The ring glittered if she but moved, and Hanne moved a great deal.

Miriam sat rocking in the rocking chair, thankful that Hanne was talking so that she wouldn't have to talk herself.

Rolf was coming on leave. She was going to see him again for the first time since the war had ended, and still she sat there so listless . . . empty and queer inside. Rolf, who wrote such sweet letters. While they didn't make her happy, they were like a bandage on a sore, a cool hand on a hot forehead. No more, no less.

"And we'll marry before Terje has finished," Hanne went on. "We'll have one room or an apartment. Are you listening to me?"

"Yes, you're going to get married before Terje has finished and live in one room or an apartment."

"I've probably told you all this before, maybe much too often. But where will we find a place to live? Mother and Father are so happy that you and Ole Jacob are here, so they won't be alone. But where on earth are Terje and I to find a place of our own!"

Strangers were now living in the little home for which Agda and Georg had risked their lives. Their precious belongings had been plundered by the German soldiers. They had carried off all the pretty things which had been purchased after such endless reflection and deliberation. Miriam sat in the rocking chair and remembered how she and Agda had "talked house" until everyone else asked them to "please shut up," and they had stopped for five minutes only to start again. Not a chair, not a plate, not a spoon was left from all these talked-over things. Not a garment, and . . . and not even Georg and Agda. It was as though the two who had loved each other so dearly had never existed.

"Miriam!" Hanne came over and knelt in front of the rocking chair, and rested her arms on her friend's lap. "Miriam, can't you try to think a little less? Talk a little more instead? Especially today with Rolf coming. You can't just sit and rock."

"No," said Miriam.

"The two of you should get married. It's the only sensible thing to do."

"Oh, Hanne, I don't know. I don't know if I'm in love with him. I can't seem to remember what he looks like even. I'm so numb!"

"Wait until you see him, then you'll know if you're in love with him all right," said Hanne from experience. "Tell me a little about his last letter."

"He wrote that his father and mother are back in their apartment again, but it looks terrible. Mrs. Kjeldsen just cleans and cleans."

Hanne laughed.

"I believe that. And pretties up and pretties down. Pillows here and lampshades there."

Miriam thought of Rolf's mother. Dainty, capricious. In reality, Miriam had never stopped longing for Mrs. Kjeldsen, for the comfort and beauty in the air around her. She was, if not always kind, at least indulgent. If Miriam and Rolf continued to be friends, Mrs. Kjeldsen would probably put up with her just as she tolerated the spots on Rolf's clothing . . .

"Now you're brooding again!" Hanne shook her friend gently. "You're going to *talk,* I tell you. What else does Rolf say?"

"He says his mother hopes I'll come and help her."

"See! See! She's improving."

In other words, Miriam thought, she had been promoted from being tolerated to being wanted. She would have to bring Rolf's mother some flowers to replace the bouquet she had never received. If she could bear meeting her again. She was such poor company nowadays with her thoughts leading in only one direction. To gas chambers and all the horrors the newspapers wrote about.

Hanne shook her.

"You're thinking about sad things!"

Miriam forced a smile. "I'll try, Hanne. I'll really try."

"Now we'll go downstairs and get the house ready before Rolf comes! There are still flowers in the garden which aren't shedding too much. Suppose you and Ole Jacob arrange the flowers. I'll help Mother with the food. She wants to have a party. Miriam, dear, you must pull yourself together!"

"Can't you understand that that's just what I must stop doing. I have to start *feeling* again. Good and bad."

"I think you'll feel good when Rolf comes. What else did he write?"

"He wrote . . . he wrote . . ." Miriam pulled the letter from her pocket, "that Papa hasn't died in vain. That now, at any rate, people must understand what racial prejudice can lead to. How terrible it is."

"How true, how true. Rolf can really put it in words. You'll be getting quite a fellow for a husband. Come on now."

At the desk in the parlor, Ole Jacob sat tinkering with cogwheels and tiny screws. The clock on the mantelpiece had stopped. A sound was missing in the room. The clock *must* tick when Rolf came.

The sun hung low, making crooked squares on the rug. But it was so warm that the veranda door stood wide open.

Miriam left Ole Jacob sitting with his mantelpiece clock, while she went mechanically in and out with the flowers and budding branches, without any joy in the flowers or anything else. There was still an hour left before Rolf would arrive and Ole Jacob would certainly have the clock ticking by then. It was good to see him so eager and busy, then he couldn't think about gas chambers and about the five hundred Norwegian Jews, of whom only twelve had returned.

It didn't help to brood, Hanne had said. That didn't bring anyone back to life.

Rolf was coming around seven o'clock.

She went out to the pantry and found vases for the flowers.

Voices could be heard from the kitchen. Apparently Mrs. Hoygard had a friend with her. Miriam hoped she wouldn't stay for supper. Now Miriam worked quietly so she wouldn't have to speak to someone she didn't know. She put the vases on the table and started to arrange the flowers in them.

"Sweet children," the strange voice was saying. "You would hardly know they're Jews."

Miriam ran the water in the vases silently.

"But after all it *is* kind of you to take them into the house. I must say that."

"Not at all," said Mrs. Hoygard tartly. "Not kind one bit. Just nice to have them."

"Yes, but there *is* something about the Jews," the voice persisted. "They're so . . . different. I can't say I like them. There's nothing I can do about it."

Quickly Miriam shut the door to the parlor. Ole Jacob mustn't hear this.

A discussion had arisen out in the kitchen; she heard Hanne's thin, excited voice. Oh, thank goodness Hanne was out there!

"Well, there's really nothing I can do about thinking it," said the voice.

"Maybe you can't do anything about thinking it, but you can do something about *saying* it, at any rate," said Hanne. Her voice had gotten a trace of a Trondheim accent. "Such opinions are more contagious than measles or colds!"

"But I'm not saying anything wrong about these two here," the voice defended itself. "It's about . . . well, about the Jews in general."

"Think a little bit about what the Jews in general have had to go through in these times! Shouldn't we carry them on thrones of gold . . . shouldn't we . . ."

Hanne was going strong. Miriam didn't have to stand there any longer.

Silently she opened the door to the parlor, wondering how she would comfort Ole Jacob. It was quite still over in their father's high-backed chair by the desk. Miriam couldn't see him. She racked her brain, trying to think of something to take away the sting of what he had heard. It was difficult to talk to Ole Jacob about unjust prejudice. He preferred not to say anything.

Miriam, pretending to be on an errand, headed over towards the open veranda door and glanced casually over at him.

Ole Jacob was asleep.

His head lay on his arm, and his arm lay right in the midst of a jumble of cogwheels and screws. The late afternoon sun was shining right on him, but he slept undisturbed, with an expression of peace and contentment on his face.

The sight of Ole Jacob made her calmer.

Silently she ran up the stairs to the attic, fixed her hair in front of the mirror without really knowing what she was doing. As she tightened the belt around her waist, her hand shook.

What hurt so much was that otherwise nice, decent people said things like that.

"More contagious than measles or colds," Hanne had said. Then decent people probably caught it too.